A LOVE SO GOOD- THE CHAMBER BROTHERS 2

K. RENEE

Chapter One

ZOEY

y heart is broken, and I don't even know how to process what has happened. Cas and I came back to her house last night after Priest put me out. Thank God she didn't contact the landlord about her moving out. This shit had me feeling like my world has been turned upside down. We haven't heard anything from anyone in the Chamber family, and I was going crazy not knowing what was going on with Sasha. Well, I guess we wouldn't hear anything if they're accusing me of hurting her. I would never hurt her, and I thought he trusted me with her. The look on his face and him holding the gun to my head kept flashing through my mind. I just knew that he was going to kill me over something that I didn't do.

"Zoey, how are you feeling?" Cas asked as she walked into the room.

"I'm so fucking hurt I can't even think straight right now. I can't believe that he would think I did some shit like that to her, Cas. I swear I would never hurt that little girl; I love her too much to even think of hurting her," I cried.

"I know, baby. I believe you, and I promise we gone get to the bottom of this shit. I'm mad as fuck right now. I know they better not come over here with no shit because I'm ready for they ass. Fuck that love shit! We family and you gone always come first, especially when a muthafucka accusing you of some shit you wouldn't think of doing. I can't get over that shit. I mean, that entire scene the last night was fucked up!" Cas was mad as hell.

"Cas, I don't want you to go through nothing with Nas because of me. He was only taking up for his brother," I told her.

"Fuck that! And I'm only taking up for you. They don't get to just pull a gun on you and think that shit sweet. I'm fuckin' a nigga up, and that's my muthafuckin' word. You need to eat, Zoey. You haven't eaten anything. You didn't even eat the breakfast I made you this morning, and we not about to do that shit up in here." I understand what she was saying, but I haven't had an appetite, and it was just hard to even think about eating.

"Cas, I will try and eat later. Do you think it's a way for us to find out if Sasha is doing alright? I really need to know if she's okay," I cried, I just couldn't control the tears and all I wanted to do was hold her.

"I'm not sure how we would get any information. I know

for sure the hospital won't give us anything on her. I will do my best to get some information for you, I promise. Now get up and go take a shower. By the time you're done, I should have some food ready for you. Zoey, everything is going to be alright. You just have to stand strong on this shit. I know you love Priest and Sasha, but you have to think about you right now. And letting yourself spiral into a deep depression is not gone work for me. I will not let you do that shit to yourself; I don't give a fuck who it is," Cas said and walked out of the room.

I grabbed my phone and pulled up all the pictures that I had of Sasha and I just cried. I cried because I wanted her to be alright. I sent up a prayer for her and went to go take my shower. Cas was right; I needed to try and pull myself together. Stepping into the shower and letting the warm water cascade down my body felt amazing. Priest's face flashed into my head, and I couldn't hold it, I broke down. I cried so much until I was heaving, I just couldn't pull it together it was heartbreaking. I can't believe that this shit was happening to me, to us. I wanted this nightmare to go the fuck away. I finally got my shit together and took my shower. Walking back into the bedroom, I saw that Cas had laid a fresh pair of pajamas on the bed for me. I didn't have anything with me. We got out of Priest's house so fast I wasn't able to grab any of my clothes. Once I was dressed, I walked out and sat down at the table.

"I'm making some burgers and fries; I know that's your favorite. I will be right back, let me put the fries on the plate." She sat a Pepsi in front of me and went back into the kitchen. A few minutes later, she came out with both of our plates, and we sat to eat dinner.

"Zoe, grab the remote and turn the television on." As soon as I turned the television on something caught my eye on the news.

"Cas, look!" I yelled.

"What the fuck?! It was a shooting at Bianca's!" Cas jumped up.

"Oh my God! They said the owner was shot last night and in critical condition," I said, throwing my hands over my mouth.

"Damn, that's Kash. I pray that he will be okay. He is such a cool ass man, and he has been through so much," Cas said, shaking her head.

"I can't believe this, first Sasha and now, Kash. I'm sure they are all going through a tough time right now." Even though I was treated like shit, my heart still goes out to the family. Cas and I sat and ate our lunch, but I couldn't even get half of it down. I just didn't have an appetite right now. I sent up a prayer for Kash. I really hope he pulls through this.

Chapter Two

PRIEST

*W*e were sitting at the hospital playing the waiting game, praying that my Pop wakes up. They said he was shot three times twice in the chest and once in the stomach. All the bullets exited his body, but one of the bullets caused some damage to his stomach and a blood vessel. Because the vessel was hit, they had to repair it and stop the bleeding. He also has a lot of tissue damage. They said it's a 50/50 chance that he may pull through this. That shit was tearing us up. I need for my fuckin' dad to wake the fuck up.

"Man, this shit is fuckin' crazy! I know who did this shit, and I promise you once I know that Pop is gone be alright, I'm going to kill that nigga and his bitch! Lonnie said she came into the restaurant, and Pop walked out with her. He said the next thing he knew, people were screaming and running into the restaurant." Nas was not in a good space, and I was right there with him.

"I just need for you boys to be careful; my baby is back there fighting for his life. My great granddaughter is in the hospital fighting for her life. I don't need shit to happen to you two. I know what you're into and I know you're going to retaliate. Just be careful out there. Priest, is Zoey with Sasha?" Big mama asked. Everything has been going so damn fast I didn't tell her what was going on.

"Big mama, they found arsenic poison in Sasha's blood," I said to her.

"Oh my lord. Somebody tried to kill my grandbaby?" She questioned, as the tears filled her eyes.

"Yeah, I got the call while you were up there with her. Right after that, we got the call about Pop. Big mama, Zoey won't be around us anymore. When the hospital called, they said that they believed it was spoon-fed to her, because of the levels in her body. I immediately went and searched the house to see if it was any traces of the shit in my house. I found it in Zoey's bedroom, in her closet," I told her.

"Wait, what? You actually believe that Zoey did this to Sasha?" She asked. I would have never thought that this bitch could do some shit like this, but the proof was there.

"It's fucked up, but I swear it's got to be more to the story, bro. We're talking about Zoey here, she loves Sasha. I'm down to do whatever you need, and I will always ride with you and for you. I just don't know about this. For some reason I think we need to look deeper into this shit. I don't think it should have gone as far as putting a gun to her head and kicking her out of the house," Nas spoke shaking his head." I know I put Nas in a fucked-up situation with Cas, but this was my fucking daughter we're talking about.

"You did what?! Lord, I know damn well you didn't do that to that girl. What the fuck is wrong with you niggas?! Just because the shit was in her closet, don't mean that she put the shit there. I have watched that girl interact with Sasha; she was willing to go to jail when that bitch Keisha messed with them at the mall. You didn't think to look at any of this shit before you just put a gun to her head?" She questioned.

"When it comes to my child, I will do anything to protect her. I found the shit in her room, not the staff quarters, and my staff has been with us for a while. None of this didn't happen until Zoey came. Right now, my concern is getting her better and making sure Pop is good! Once that happens, I will get to the bottom of all of this shit. I don't want her near my child, and that shit is final." I meant what I said. They don't have to understand what I'm going through right now.

If it was their child, and someone called telling them that their kid had been poisoned, what the fuck would they have done? Especially if they found the shit on someone that lives in their house. Seriously, what the fuck would you do? I'm not trying to hear that shit from them right now. I decided to go back over to Chop and check on my daughter. Good thing is that my dad was at the University of Pennsylvania hospital, and it was right near Chop. When I made it up to Sasha's room, the nurse was checking her vitals. Her fever had started to break. Since they knew what was causing her sickness, now they were able to treat her. I gave my statement to child protective services, and before they can release Sasha to me, they had to come out to the home. Thank God they still let me be with her, but a nurse was in the room 24/7 now.

They wanted information on all the people that had access to her. They spoke to Nas already, and they would eventually talk to Big mama. I gave them the phone numbers to all the staff that worked for me, and of course, I gave them Zoey's number. They could investigate this shit all they wanted to, but once my investigation was done, it's gone be a murder right after it.

"Mr. Chamber, Dr. Taylor needs to speak with you. I will let him know that you're back," the nurse said to me and walked out. About ten minutes later, Dr. Taylor came into the room.

"Mr. Chamber, I hope everything is going to be alright with your father? I know this is a difficult time for you, but I have some more discouraging news. It seems that because of the arsenic poison, Sasha has developed a bad case of anemia. Her blood levels are low, and she needs a blood transfusion. Of course, the donor must be a match to her, and we need to try and get this done as soon as possible," he stated, and I was ready to give my blood.

"I'm ready, let's get this done." I would give my baby all the damn blood in my body if I had to.

"First, we have to test your blood to make sure you're a match. Sasha's blood type is O positive and the donor needs to be O as well. Do you know your blood type?" Dr. Taylor questioned.

"I'm B positive, but you can still check my blood. I will have the rest of my family come to see if they're a match," I said to him.

"Hmmm, that's interesting. Are you sure you're B positive?" He asked.

"Yes, I'm sure, but you can check me out to be sure." I wanted them to hurry and get this shit done.

"Ok, let's get you tested, and make sure you get the mother here to be tested as well," he said, and that means I had to find Keisha. I called Nas and asked that he and Big mama come over to get tested. He said they were on their way, and I was relieved. By the time I was finished getting tested, Nas and Big mama had shown up, and they took them back to be tested as well. Nas called Cannon and asked him to get Keisha and bring her up to the hospital to be tested.

"They want us all to wait here until they run all the tests to see if we're a match." This shit was making me nervous. My baby needed us, and we were her family, so one of us have to be able to help her.

"What the fuck did you do to my daughter?" Keisha came into the room with her fucked-up ass attitude.

"She needs a blood transfusion, and you need to act like you got some fuckin' sense." I got in her face.

"Ma'am, if you follow me, I will take you to get tested," the nurse said and led her out of the room. It took about twenty minutes for Keisha to come back, and now we all just have to wait. Two hours had passed before the doctor came into Sasha's room.

"We tested everyone's blood type, and no one is a match to Sasha," he said, and we were all sitting here in shock and confused as hell.

"What the fuck does that mean? Both of her parents are here, at least one of them has to be a match for her!" Nas shouted.

"One would think that, and in most cases, it's true, just not in this case. I found it strange because I've never experienced that before. But we can get into those questions and answers later. Right now, my need to find a blood match for Sasha is much more important. Now we may have an O donor blood here in the hospital bank, and we're checking that out. If there is anyone else that you can think of, please get them down here," Dr. Taylor stated and walked out of the room. It was funny to me that the entire time Keisha was in the room, she hasn't said anything to Sasha. She didn't even attempt to go to her bedside and say hello.

Chapter Three

CASSIE

I felt so bad for Zoey. She was really going through it. I can't believe Priest did this shit to her. I was ready to beat that nigga's ass. I get it and understand that he's going through some shit, but don't accuse her of doing no shit like that without proof. I'm mad as hell at Nas for even following that bullshit up. That nigga can kiss my ass right now. He's been calling my damn phone and I've been sending his ass straight to voicemail. Fuck them niggas, that's the way I'm feeling and that's what the fuck it's gone be. I feel so fucked up about Kash being shot, and I wanted to call Big mama so bad to check on him. It's killing me to hear Zoey in there crying her heart out for Sasha, and I know some of those tears were for Priest as well. They would've been good for each other, and I hope that he fixes this shit. For now, I'm riding with my cousin, and I'm not fucking budging until them niggas figure it the fuck out. I heard my phone ringing and I ran into my room to grab it.

"Hello," I didn't recognize the number.

"Hi, Cassie. This is Bella, I'm Tamara's attorney from Blu Cosmetics. We received your concerns and I've sent over a new contract for Zoey. We are in agreeance with her doing other work, except for cosmetic deals. Also, the launch date has been moved up and we are wondering if she can make her way to New York, by Friday to get herself situated. We've already set up her living accommodations, and we will begin shooting for the campaign on Tuesday. Everything is in the email that I sent you. Once she signs it, we will have the amount we agreed on, delivered to her when she arrives in New York," Bella stated, and I was sitting here with my damn mouth wide open.

"Yes, she will be there. I will look over everything, and if it's in order, we will get it signed and see you all at the shoot." I hung up with her, jumping up and down in excitement. This shit was crazy. These people were pulling out all of the stops to get Zoey. I was sitting here reading over the contract, and they were paying her a million dollars, travel expenses, food, and paying for living expenses for a brownstone on the Upper Westside of Manhattan. Damn, my cousin just glowed up on they ass, and I can't wait to see her shine like a muthafuckin diamond. I walked into her bedroom, and she was lying there in tears.

"Zoey, I need for you to shake this shit off. I just got a call from Blu Cosmetics' attorney, and they agreed to our counter.

You can work with other companies just as long as it's not cosmetics. They got you a place in New York. They had to move the date of the launch up and need you there by Friday so that you're prepared for the shoot that starts on Tuesday," I told her, as I showed her the email.

"What?! They're doing all of that and paying me the money? Wait, I can't leave. I need to know what's going on with Sasha before I leave," she said.

"Zoey, I know that you love her, I love her too. However, even if you stayed here, he doesn't want you near his daughter. Maybe one day you can work things out, but right now, this should be about you. Your life is about to change for the better, and you did this shit on your own. This is something you have to do for yourself, baby girl." I had to get that through her head that it was time to start living for Zoey. My phone started going off, and I went to grab it. I was shocked as hell to see that it was Big mama.

"Hey, Big mama, I'm so sorry to hear about Kash. Zoey and I saw it on the news, and we sent up a prayer for him. How are you holding up?" I asked her, as I placed the call on speaker and walked back into the room with Zoe.

"Things could be better, but we're going through a rough time right now, baby. I know what happened, and I'm mad as hell at that boy for what he did. He should have checked things out before accusing that child of this mess. Listen, things have gotten bad for Sasha. She needs to have a blood transfusion, and I need for y'all to get tested to see if you can help her. She is an O type, and these people are saying that only an O blood type can donate to her," Big mama cried, and my heart went out to her.

"My blood type is O positive. Maybe I can donate to her," Zoey spoke, jumping out of bed.

"Big mama, we're on our way down there, but if Priest gives us a problem, I'm beating his ass," I said to her, and I meant that shit.

"Don't you worry about them; I will help you beat his ass. I got my bible ready and waiting to give his ass the word. Y'all just come on up to the room when you get here," Big mama stated, and we ended the call. It took us about thirty minutes to get down to Chop, we signed in and headed up to Sasha's room. Walking into the room all eyes were on us, and Priest snapped.

"Didn't I tell you to stay the fuck away from us!" He yelled, and tears filled Zoey's eyes.

"You better not drop not nan muthafuckin' tear for this nigga," I whispered to her, as I held her hand.

"Boy, sit your ass down somewhere! They're here because I called them up here. You're being a rude, nasty nigga and this child might be the one to save your damn daughters life! Now sit yo' ass down and shut the fuck up!" Big mama snapped. Nas was staring at me, and I stuck my middle finger up at his ass. Fuck that nigga, I'm not playing with none of these niggas today.

"Big mama, where do I go?" Zoey asked.

"Nurse, she would like to be tested. Can you help them out, please?" Big mama asked the nurse, and she escorted us out of the room. Priest looked like he was ready to burst, but who gives a damn. Once Zoey and I both got tested, we went back to the room, but we decided to stand outside of the room and wait. The doctor came running down the hall and into the room.

"Mr. Chamber, Zoey Matthews, she just tested as a positive match. Is she still here?" The doctor questioned.

"I'm Zoey Matthews," she said as she walked into the room.

"Ms. Matthews, are you willing to donate to baby Sasha?" He asked her.

"Yes, sir." Zoey could barely get her answer out because she was crying so hard.

"Good. Follow me and we will get you all set up," he stated, and led Zoey out of the room. I was standing outside the door, and Nas walked out and stood in front of me.

"Cas, we need to talk." I know this nigga ain't standing in my face with that let's talk bullshit.

"That was the shit you should have said to me when you let your brother treat my cousin like shit," I said to him.

"Cas, there was a lot of shit going on, and everyone was just too upset to think on some rational shit. I told Priest that he needs to look into this shit further, but I need you right now, ma. My Pops and niece are all fucked up, and I need my girl," he said to me.

"Look, I'm sorry to hear about your dad, and I'm praying for him. Right now, that girl has been going through hell. You have your family to be with you and tell you everything is going to be alright. She has nobody because the lil' family she thought she was gaining, that nigga shitted on her," I told him.

"Do you, lil' mama, but know I'm coming for my girl sooner or later. I will give you the time you need for now." He walked back into the room. All this shit is fucked up because I really love that dude and I was looking forward to our life together. A couple of hours later, Zoe came walking down the hall with the nurse.

"Hey, are you alright?" I asked her.

"Yeah, do you think they will let me see her? I just want to tell her I love her," Zoe looked at me with tears in her eyes me.

"Hell yeah, you can see her after what you just did for her. I wish a nigga would say you can't see her, come on." I grabbed her hand and we walked into the room.

"Zoey would like to speak to Sasha," I stated, and Big mama stood up.

"Come on, baby. She's resting, but you can see her." Big mama grabbed Zoe's hand and they both walked to Sasha's bed.

"Hey, Sash, I miss you, baby girl. I think about you every minute of the day, and I'm praying you feel better soon. I love you always," Zoey cried as she rubbed her hand.

"Ma-ma," Sasha said clear as day, and that just broke Zoey's ass down.

"See you around, baby," she whispered and rushed out of the room. I walked out behind her and we left the hospital.

"You alright?" I asked, looking over at her.

"Yeah, I'm just ready to leave and get my life together. The doctor has my number, and if he needs me, he will call me. I told him that I'm leaving in two days, but if there is an emergency and I need to come back, I would."

I picked up dinner, and we went home, and for the first time, Zoey ate all of her food. I hope that this move will make her feel better and bring happiness back into her life.

$\mathcal{I}$ meant what I said to Cassie, I'm coming for my fuckin' girl. I understand why she was pissed, but like I said, tensions were high that night. I had to rock out with my brother and try to get his ass to calm the fuck down. There was no way that I would've let him hurt Zoey because I didn't believe that she would harm, Sasha. Believe me, once we get this family shit under control, we gone find out what happened. I know that nigga Ronnie had something to do with my Pop getting hit. I decided to come back over here and sit in my Pop's room with him. The rest of the family is over at Chop with Sasha. They were getting ready to do the blood transfusion. Priest needs to wake the hell up, why would Zoey come to save his daughter if she tried to kill her? Looking at my dad lying here with all these damn tubes in him, had a nigga fucked up. That nigga

Ronnie can count his muthafuckin' days because I'm killing his bitch ass.

"Pop, you got to wake up, man. We need you. Mom left us; you can't leave us too. You have to pull through this shit, you a Chamber, and we don't fall easy. You don't have to worry we gone get that nigga for you, I put my life on that shit," I told him, as I cried. Kashas Chamber was one of the realest men I've ever known. He raised us to be just like him. I loved this dude, and I'm gone paint the city of New York red over my fuckin Pop.

"Hello," a woman softly spoke, as she knocked and walked into the room.

"Stepmama, come on in," I spoke, kind of surprised to see her here.

"I hope it's ok that I stopped by. We had a thank-you date setup and when I went to the restaurant, Lonnie told me what happened. He said he didn't think it would be a problem if I came by to see him," she said, as she walked up to his bedside.

"Nah, it's no problem. My nigga doing bad right now, so don't hold nothing against him. If his breath or his armpits stank, you better still be his girl." I laughed.

"You are something else. Now what makes you think I don't already have a man or husband for that matter?" She asked.

"Well, if you do, that nigga is gone have to move around. 'Cause I already claimed you as my stepmama, and my pop needs a real stallion like you in his life. Another thing, I can't be claiming no ugly ass step mama. My step mama, gotta be bad as hell, so I can brag about her," I told her, and we burst into laughter.

"I will let him know," she said, and started talking to Pop.

"Kash, this is Eva. You have to wake up, so you can take me on that thank you dinner you promised me. I hope this wasn't your way of getting out of it, because I won't let you," Eva said, just as Priest and Big mama walked into the room.

"Hey, Ms. Eva. How are you?" Priest spoke to her.

"Hey, Priest. I'm sorry about your father. Hello, my name is Eva Jackson. I'm Kashas' decorator," she introduced herself to Big mama.

"Oh, how you doing? Thank you for stopping by to see my son. Just keep him in your prayers because he's going to need it," Big mama told her.

"Big mama, this is me and Priest stepmama. This gone be Pop new wife, and yo' daughter in law." I smiled.

"Well, at least she pretty, and this nigga need to get some," Big mama stated.

"Say that shit, Big mama!" I shook my head because Pop does need to get him some ass when he wakes up.

"You two are so damn embarrassing," Priest spoke.

"And you a dummy, so what's your point!" When Big mama said that shit, I fell out laughing. We all sat around and talked for a little while, and Eva was a cool chick. Priest left and went back to be with Sasha. I hope that Pop comes out of this shit soon because this family needed him.

Chapter Five

KASH

I could see her so clear; she was wearing a white dress, and the sun shined so bright against her beautiful skin.

"Kashas, wake your ass up and get back to my sons. I love you, and I will always love you, but this is not your time. You still have your life to live, and so much love to give her. She's beautiful, and I think you two would make a beautiful couple. Take care of my babies and tell them that mommy loves them." Bianca turned to walk away.

"Bianca! Bianca! No don't leave! Come back to me, baby!" I screamed her name over and over again. The bright sunlight dimmed, and I could hear beeping sounds.

"You think that nigga going coma crazy? Why is he screaming and moving around in the bed like that?" I heard a voice say.

"Nah, maybe them drugs got his ass going a little cuckoo," I heard my mother's voice, and I tried to open my eyes. When I tried again, my eyes popped open, and Nas and my mother jumped back.

"Yoooo, Pop, the next time you want to wake up like you had an acting part in The Living Dead, let my thug ass know. You almost got yo' ass knocked back into that coma you was in. Wake yo' ass up like regular people do when they been in a coma, slow and muthafuckin' easy," Nas said, shaking his head at me.

"I know that's right. I just pulled my damn heart out my ass. Kashas, welcome back, baby. I'm so happy you're awake." My mother held my hand, and I squeezed her hand because I knew she was worried to death.

"I'm going out here to tell them that you're awake," Nas said and walked out of the room. A few minutes later, the nurses and doctor came in to do an exam on me. Once they were complete, they pulled the tube out of my mouth. My throat was on fire, so Nas poured me a cup of water and held it up to my mouth for me to drink.

"How long have I been here?" I asked. My voice was a little raspy, and my throat was sore as hell.

"A few days. I will call Priest and let him know that you're up. He's over at the hospital with Sasha," Nas stated.

"How is she? Why is she still there?" I asked him.

"Pop, it's a long story, and we will fill you in on that later. I'm just glad to see you up, and now it's time for you to heal. I'm putting someone in this room with you at all times. We both know who did this shit, and now that you're up and on the road to recovery, I can make some muthafuckin' noise in these streets," Nas said. I was going to have to talk to him. because I wanted to wait until I was completely back to normal before we made a move. I definitely want to get at this nigga myself, and of course, I knew my sons would ride this out with me. I know his ass is going to get comfortable and that's exactly what I want him to do. Once I'm released, I will go home and start my healing process. I know if I rest and not overdo it, I will get better faster. My fuckin' bullets will be the only bullets that will take Ronnie and his bitch out.

"Damn, it's good to see you up. You had me stressed the fuck out and ready to cause a bloodbath around these fuckin' parts," Dame said as he walked into the room.

"It's good to see you, bro," I whispered, and he dapped me up. Priest came running into the room, and I smiled at my oldest son. I knew he was going through a tough time being since I was here, and Sasha was in the hospital too.

"Sup, son? It's good to see you," I spoke, as he grabbed my hand.

"You have no idea how good it is to hear your voice, Pop. I love you, and I'm glad to see you up." He smiled.

"Where is Zoey? I hope I didn't miss our game of backgammon," I said to him. On Wednesday nights, Zoey and I enjoyed a couple of games of backgammon with some dessert.

"Pop, I hate to tell you this, you gone need to find you another backgammon partner. Because this nigga threw your original partner away." Nas was shaking his head, and I looked over at Priest.

"What? What happened to Zoe?" I questioned, just as my room door opened, and Eva walked in.

"Hello, everyone. Kash, it's so good to see you up," she said, walking up to the bed and touched my hand.

"Eva, thank you. I'm surprised to see you here." I smiled.

"I was here yesterday. I thought you stood me up so I asked Lonnie, and he told me what happened," she said, as Nas gave her a chair to sit in.

"It's good to see you, Eva," my mother spoke to her, and that shit surprised me. Because my mama always had some smart shit to say out of her mouth.

"Same here, Ms. Chamber." Eva smiled.

"Stepmama, Pop gone need a bath soon. That nigga ain't washed in a couple of days, his balls might be a little sweaty. Just remember what I said, you better not hold that shit against him," Nas told her, and I swear if I had the strength I would body slam this nigga. Priest shook his head, and Eva just laughed.

"Son, we need to talk later about Zoey," I told Priest, I didn't want his ass to think that he didn't have to explain what happened. His ass damn sure gone have to tell me what was up. Zoey was such a sweet girl. I knew it was going to take some time for me to heal, but I'm happy as hell that I was blessed with a second chance at life.

Chapter Six
ZOEY

Seeing him broke me, but being able to help Sasha meant so much to me. Even though I was leaving a piece of my heart behind me, I knew that nothing good would come from being here right now. I'm glad that I will be able to call Big mama and check on Sasha. Knowing that made me feel so much better. The social worker from child protective service just left, and I answered all the questions she had for me. I did tell her that it was no way that Priest would hurt Sasha. The good thing that came from that conversation is that I don't think she believes I did it. She didn't come out and say it. It was just the way she talked to me. I told her about my modeling career and asked that she keep it confidential. She said if she needed anything else, she would call me.

"Are you ready to get out of here?" Cas asked.

"Yep, let's do this." We walked out of the house heading to New York. I felt a sadness come over me, and it just emotionally took over my body. Cas didn't say anything; she just held my hand and let me cry it all out.

"Cas, promise me that you will forgive Nas. He is stuck in a really hard place right now. The way he looks at you, I can tell that he loves you. I'm not saying you have to forgive him today, but promise you will give him a chance to explain his side of it all. He stopped Priest from hurting me. If he wasn't there to talk him down, I'm not sure what would have happened. I know you're mad at him, you both deserve happiness. Promise me, Cassie." I could see it all over her the other day at the hospital, how much she missed him. She was trying to be hard and protect me and I love her for that. I just didn't want her to give up her happiness for me.

"I promise, at some point, I will give him an opportunity to talk." She smiled. A couple of hours later, we were pulling up to the brownstone in the Upper Westside of Manhattan. When the company liaison asked my desired living arrangement, I told them I didn't want to be in an apartment building. So, they found me a brownstone to live in, and I will be here for at least a year.

"Damn, even the outside of this shit is nice." Cas and I were both admiring the place. It was on a really nice block. The realtor is meeting us here so that she could show me around and give me the keys. Cas and I grabbed our bags and headed inside. Ringing the doorbell, we waited, hoping that she was already here.

"Hi, can I help you?" She questioned.

"Hi, my name is Zoey Matthews, I'm supposed to move in today."

"Yes, Ms. Matthews, I have been expecting your arrival. Come on in and I can show you around," she stated.

"Ok, thanks," I said to her.

"Ms. Matthews, here is a folder with all of the nearby restaurants, grocery stores, pharmacies, and the closest hospital," Teresa stated as we walked around the house. Cas and I were both looking at this place in pure amazement. It was beautiful.

"This is beautiful, my God. I would have never expected a Brownstone to look like this," I told her.

"Yes, ma'am, it is thirty-five hundred square ft. of luxury living. Blu Cosmetics stated that they wanted nothing but the best for you. Upstairs you have three bedrooms and three bathrooms. Two of the bedrooms have a bathroom, and the other bathroom is across the hall from the third bedroom. On the first level, you have a spacious living room, and off to the left here, you have a full bar room. The entire house is equipped with surround sound. If you need help with anything, I'm available to you until your lease ends," Teresa stated.

"Thank you," I told her. The doorbell sounded off, and Teresa walked off to answer the door.

"Zoey, a courier is here for you." I walked to the door, and the guy handed me an envelope. I signed for it and he left.

"I'm going to get out of here and let you ladies get settled in. Your keys, code to the alarm, and code to the door keypad are all in the folder I gave you," Teresa stated, and we said our goodbyes.

"Look at you! Babbbby, this shit right here is dope as hell. I guess homegirl wanted you bad, 'cause that heifer got you living it up in here! Now, let's look at this damn check to see if the numbers are right," Cas spoke. We were expecting the courier to come by sometime today with my check. I opened the envelope, and the check was for five hundred thousand dollars. We knew that I would get the other half of the payment in installments, but I was fine with that. I have never in my entire fuckin' life had this type of money before. I handed it to Cas, and she was dancing all around the damn living room.

"Cas, this shit feels like a dream." I looked at her, and this heifer pinched me.

"Ouch! What the hell you do that for?" I laughed, rubbing my damn arm.

"To let your ass know that this isn't a damn dream. This is real muthafuckin' life, boo, and I'm so happy for you." I wanted to deposit this check and go buy myself some clothes. There was so much that I needed since I never tried to go get my clothes from Priest's house. Cas and I went up to take a look at our bedrooms then decided to head out to deposit this check and to do some shopping. Since Cas is not working for Priest anymore, which was totally her decision, she's decided to stay up here with me for a while. She said she will go back to Philadelphia at some point.

"Cas, I think I need to buy me a car," I told her. When I was staying with Priest, he gave me a car to drive, but shit has changed and now I need a car.

"We can go out and look for one tomorrow. Unless you want to wait until next weekend," she stated.

"Next weekend is fine. You're here, so there is no big rush for it." I knew I would have to get one soon, but I was cool with waiting for a little while.

Cassie and I never discussed her pay for being my manager. I asked the bank to courier over a check for fifty thousand dollars as soon as the money clears my account. I plan to give her more, but for now, this was a token of my appreciation. By the time we made it back in, it was damn near ten. Walking into my bedroom, I needed a warm shower to ease the tension in my body. I told Cas I would meet her downstairs so that we could go inside the bar room and have a drink. My cell phone was ringing, and I had to dig in my purse to grab it. It was from a blocked number.

"Hello... Hello? Hello?" There was silence on the other end, and then the line went dead. I guess they had the wrong number, but for some reason, Priest instantly came to mind. I'm sure it wasn't him because he hated my ass and didn't want shit to do with me. I put the clothes away that I bought today and hopped into the shower. I could get used to this. The best feeling about all of this is no man helped me get to this point in my life. Even though I'm in my feelings about Priest and Sasha, I could see light at the end of this dark ass tunnel for me.

I was sitting here with Sasha. Since the blood transfusion, she was doing so much better. I sat back and took in some of the things that my family was saying. If Zoey did this to Sasha, why would she be the one to save her life? I have been thinking about that shit all damn day. My staff has been with me for a long time and I thought I could trust them. The only reason I flew off the handle with Zoey is that all the evidence pointed to her. I picked the phone up so many times, wanting to call her but never did. Until tonight, I called to say thank you for what she did to save my baby. When she answered and said hello a few times, I just hung up. I needed to get to the bottom of this shit, because if Zoey didn't poison Sasha, I fucked up bad, and it's probably no coming back from that shit. Secondly, who the fuck did it if she didn't do it?

"Excuse me, I need to go home for a little while. Please don't let anyone in to see my daughter tonight, and call me if something changes with her," I said to the nurse that was sitting in the room.

"Sir, she will be perfectly fine, go home and get some rest," she stated, and I walked out to the elevators and headed home. I had no staff working until I got to the bottom of who tried to hurt my baby. I just didn't trust anyone at this point, but my immediate family. Walking into the house, I went into the kitchen to grab a bottle of water, and as I stood there looking around, the night that I had Zoey spread out all over my counter came to mind. I felt this sharp pain in my heart just thinking about it, as. As I turned to walk out of the kitchen, the small camera in the corner ceiling caught my eye. I took off running upstairs and grabbed my laptop. I forgot all about my fuckin' cameras. I had cameras in Sasha's bedroom, but I didn't have cameras in any of the other bedrooms. The good thing is that I could see if someone entered the upstairs bedrooms. I decided to go back and watch recordings for the last three months.

———

J had been watching the recordings for a couple of hours now, and I haven't seen anything out of the ordinary. I was tired as hell and needed to get some sleep, just as soon as I was getting ready to turn the recordings off for the night, I saw Jasmine talking to my housekeeper Margie.

That wouldn't have been strange to me at all because she could have asked her for something. What caused me to turn the volume up, is that it seemed as if Jasmine was talking shit to Margie.

"You need to find that damn safe, ma. We gotta hurry up and get this shit. I think he's falling for that bitch," Jasmine said to her.

"I wish you and your sister would let me handle this shit. I know what the fuck I'm doing, and I told y'all the girl was gone be a problem for us when he hired her ass," Margie said.

I couldn't believe what the fuck I was hearing. Were these bitches trying to rob my ass? And Margie is Jasmine's mama? What the fuck?! I grabbed my keys and walked out of the house as Nas was pulling in the driveway. Ever since Cas left him, he's been back staying at my house.

"You're heading back to the hospital?" He asked me.

"Nah, I'm about to go kill me a couple of bitches," I told him. He pulled his gun out and jumped in the car with me.

"I'm always ready for some action, who we going to kill?" He asked.

"I was watching some recordings from the cameras in the house. Ever since you said you didn't think Zoey had anything to do with it, it's been on my mind. So, on one of the recordings, I saw Jasmine talking to Ms. Margie, and she asked her if she found my safe and called her Ma. I think Ms. Margie is Jasmine's mother, and they were setting me up to rob me," I said to him.

"Nah, nigga, we're going back in the house and watch some more of these damn recordings. Cause if they were up to some shit, they probably did that shit to Sasha. I bet you all the money I got in the bank, and I will give up pussy for a year that them bitches had something to do with that shit. Wait, nah, I can't give up pussy for a year, because I'm gone drag my Bear back home in the next couple of weeks. I'm gone have my whole body in the pussy for at least a week. I got to make up for this pussy drought I'm on. Remind me to beat yo' ass, when shit turns normal again. Yo' ass is the reason I'm on this fuckin drought. Now come on and let's go find out who did this shit," Nas fussed, as we walked into the house.

"This shit is crazy as fuck. These bitches had it out for my ass, but I can't understand why." I looked over at Nas and he shrugged.

"There is someone else involved because Margie said you and your sister. Who the fuck is this hoe sister? Lawwd, my dick just got hard because we get to kill Jasmine's bird face, hoe ass. I'm damn sure glad it's Margie and not Ms. Carol. My heart wouldn't be able to take that shit." He was shaking his head. We were watching these recordings for hours, and the damn sun was coming up.

"Wait, go back. Look at that," I told him.

"She's going into Zoey's room, but she doesn't have anything in her hand!" I yelled.

"She doesn't have to; she could have hidden it. Margie knows you have cameras, so her old Marge Simpson looking ass wouldn't have it out in the open." Nas was right, Margie could have taken the shit into Zoey's room unnoticed.

"I'm going to kill these bitches! I have a plan. I'm going to call her and tell her she can come back to work. I'm also gone call Jasmine and tell her I need some pussy. I will tell her that Zoey and I are not together anymore." I wanted to get them here because they gone tell me the truth or I'm gone shoot that shit out of them.

"News flash nigga, you and Zoey aren't together anymore! You fucked that shit all the way up dumb ass, but the rest of that shit sounds like the move. I'm going to get some sleep, so I will be well rested when it's killing season around this bitch," Nas stated, and walked out. I took my shower and crawled into bed. I had a feeling in the pit of my stomach that I blamed and disrespected Zoey for some shit she didn't do. Fuckkkkkkkkkk!

Chapter Eight

CASSIE

We've been on set for a few hours now, and it was going on nine in the morning. They have a process that they go through, and I mean they got this shit together up in here. The stylist, makeup artist, and clothing designer have a certain amount of time to get Zoey together, and then they will start the shoot. I know she's tired because they have been pulling her left and right. One thing I can say is they had her ass looking fya as fuck right now.

"Zoe, you look amazing, I know you're gonna kill this shit today." This shoot was so different from the one we did to get her portfolio together.

"Thank you. I'm ready to get this started. I can't wait to see this all come together." She smiled, and it was time for her to get dressed. I felt my phone vibrating in my purse. Pulling it out, it was a text from Nas.

Big Dick Asshole: Morning, Bear. You got ten more days and I'm coming to get you and my pussy.

Me: I hope you know I don't live in Philly anymore, so good luck finding me.

Big Dick Asshole: Lol. You think I'm gone have my girl walking the streets of New York and I don't know where she is? I'm not sure why you're there, but believe me when I say this. I know exactly where you are, and I will see you in ten days.

I didn't even respond, because I'm trying to figure out how the fuck did he know I was in New York. *Is this stalking ass dude having me followed?* **I thought** *to myself.* About thirty minutes later, Zoey came out on set, and this girl was absolutely stunning. Some people came walking into the room, and the way everyone was running up to one of the women, I could only assume that she was the owner of Blu Cosmetics.

"Zoey, it's so good to meet you. You look amazing, and I appreciate you agreeing to take a chance with Blu Cosmetics. After this campaign, I would love to discuss future business deals." Tamara Vance was the only child to Billionaire Joseph Vance. I think her family was in the oil business. All I know is they asses was rich rich.

"Thank you, Tamara. We will be willing to entertain that just send the particulars to my manager."

Once they were done talking, the photoshoot began, and Zoey had this shit on lock. My sis did this shit effortlessly, and I was so proud to be a part of this with her. She had to do a few wardrobe changes, and with each change they also had to change her makeup to give her a different look. No matter what changes they made, she was killing the game up in this bitch tuuuday. A few hours later, they were wrapping up and going over the different looks. This shit was hard work, I can tell you that much. We've been here for damn near ten hours. By the time we made it back home, it was almost five.

"I'm so damn tired. I think I'm going to take a shower while we wait for the food."

"Ok, boo." Zoey was doing her best to act as if she was alright, but I hear her crying, and I see the shit in her eyes. She really fell hard for Priest and he did her so fuckin' bad. I'm mad as hell at him, and I do plan on going to see his ass whenever I get back to Philly. I needed to get comfortable, so I decided to jump in the shower. My mind drifted off to Nas, and I was missing him like crazy. Even though I was trying to be strong for Zoey, I was going through my own mental breakdown. I don't even know if I would call it a mental breakdown, but I was sad about not being with him. I'm pissed, and that shit is gone take some time to get over, but I still missed his fine ass. By the time I was done, the food had already arrived, and Zoey was placing the food on the table.

"Damn, that smells good." I sat down and was ready to tear my shit up. We ordered some Thai food from the restaurant down the street that we loved.

"Today was tiresome, but it was so much fun. The pictures came out so damn good, I couldn't stop staring at them. All I kept saying to myself was, damn that's me." Zoe smiled.

"Yesss! Sis, that was definitely you, and you did such an amazing job. I'm so proud of you," I said to her, as we ate our food. All of a sudden, Zoey jumped up from the table and took off running down the hall. I got up to go and check on her. I needed to make sure she was alright.

"Zoe, what's wrong?" I asked her. She was on her knees with her face damn near in the toilet, releasing the food we had just eaten. I rubbed her back to try to soothe her, but it took a few minutes. I wet a rag for her and handed it to her when she stood up.

"Cas, I don't feel well," she stated, as she kind of stumbled, and I grabbed her.

"Ohh shit, I think we need to get you checked out. Maybe the food didn't agree with you. Come on, let's get some clothes on, and I'm taking you to the emergency room." I ran up and got dressed, went into her room and grabbed her some clothes as well.

"Here, brush your teeth and get dressed. I will be in the living room waiting for you." She didn't look well at all. It took us about thirty minutes to get to the emergency room and get registered. It was packed as hell in here, and I could tell that we were going to be here for a minute. Thank God we didn't have shit to do tomorrow. About an hour later, they called Zoey back, and I went with her.

"Ms. Matthews, I'm Jackie. I need you to give me a urine sample in this cup, undress, and put this gown on. I will give you a few minutes, I'll be right back to take your vitals." Nurse Jackie walked out, and Zoey changed her gown and went to use the bathroom. Once she was done, I helped her get into bed and prayed they could give her something to make her feel better.

"I don't know what happened, but it just hit me all of a sudden. I'm so glad that you were here with me." She gave me a half-smile.

"I got you, sis. When we get home, you just need to get some rest. I think you've had too much going on in the past couple of weeks," I told her, as the nurse walked in and grabbed her urine. About forty minutes later, the doctor walked into the room.

"Ms. Matthews, I'm Dr. Warren. You state that you have been nauseated, with a little stomach pain. Is there anything else bothering you?" He asked Zoe.

"No sir, that's everything," she spoke.

"When was your last menstrual cycle?" He questioned, and it took her a minute to answer.

"Ummm, I can't remember...Uhhh, you know I don't think I got one last month," she told him, and at this point, they could just come and pick my ass up off the floor. Because a bitch done melted and slid out the chair on this shit right here.

"Mmmm, hmmm, give me one second, and I will be right back," the doctor said to her and left the room.

"Biiiihhhhhhh, you done fucked around and got pregnant by Priest muthafuckin Chamber?" I jumped up, pacing the floor.

"Cas, calm down. I don't think I'm pregnant. I never got any type of sickness with my last two pregnancies. I could just have an irregular cycle; it's not the first time that has happened to me." She shrugged.

"Girl, you got pregnant by the muthafuckin' devil before. That's why you didn't have symptoms, but you done let a different type of nigga stick his dick in you. Yo' ass gone have every system there is to let you know a Chamber baby is on the damn way," I said to her, just as the doctor walked back into the room.

"Ok, Ms. Matthews, the reason you're feeling this way is because you're pregnant. We can do a quick scan and let you know how far you are," Dr. Warren said, and Zoey just nodded. Tears filled the brim of her eyes. When they fell, I just held onto her, because I'm sure knowing that you're pregnant by the man that hates you, is a hard pill to swallow right now.

*P*riest and I were able to go over the rest of the tapes, and these bitches done fucked all the way up. We couldn't find anything showing that poison was put into Sasha's food, and I found that strange as hell. Just because we didn't see it doesn't mean their asses didn't do it. Margie old ass was due to come back to work today, and Priest and I had a plan. I was at the hospital visiting my Pop right now.

"Pop, they said if you keep improving, you get to go home soon. I'm not feeling us waiting to get at this Ronnie nigga, but this is your call, and I understand you wanting to handle that nigga yourself. You said Stormy asked you to walk her out to her car?" I wanted to know everything that he knew.

"Yeah, but she was acting weird as hell when we got outside. It was like she was trying to get away from me instead of walking with me. I think she set me up, just to get me outside. There is something else that I thought I saw, but I need to be sure on that. Once I know I will let you know. Now let's talk about this shit with Zoey. Your brother has lost his muthafuckin' mind; mama told me everything. How the fuck could he even think that she would do some shit like that?" Pop was mad as hell.

"Yeah, I know it's fucked up, but I can tell you this shit is eating him up. Because I think he's learning slowly that he fucked that shit up. I done even fucked shit up with Bear, but don't worry I got that under control," I said to him, just as Eva walked in with some food.

"I hear you," Pop said as he smiled at Eva.

"Awww, stepmama, you're bringing your boo some lunch. I like how you operate; I'm gone go and let y'all spend some time together." I said my goodbyes and headed over to Priest's house. Walking into the house, I heard laughter coming from the family room.

"Urggghhh, I haven't seen my man in months, and we just made shit official. So, we gone need some privacy tonight; we got a lot of making up to do. Right, babe?" Jasmine asked as she sipped on her drink. I was sick of this bitch already. I know we supposed to wait a while, I just don't have it in me, I'm about action and this shit ain't it.

"Bitch, fuck you, and your muthafuckin' privacy!" I pulled my gun and shot that bitch in the knee cap. Fuck that hoe; she wasn't gone be using them bitches no more anyway. If she keeps fucking talking, I'mma shoot the other one the fuck up.

"Nigga!" Priest looked from me to Jasmine as she screamed and cried in pain.

"I know we had a plan, but just looking at her hoe ass had my ass itchin' and my trigger finger jumpin'." I shrugged and walked out of the room, heading for the kitchen.

"Mr. Nas, would you like some lunch? I just put everything up, but I can make you a plate." Margie nervously smiled; I know this hoe heard that gunshot.

"Bitch, if we were the last two niggas on earth and this was the last supper, I would starve, 'cause I damn sure wouldn't eat that poisoned ass food yo' ass been in here cooking. Bring yo' ass on. You too damn old to be out here trying to set people up and kill kids and shit. I know you done fucked with the right family 'cause you ain't never gone see yours again," I roared, pulling her ass into the family room.

"Mr. Priest, I don't know what's going on," Margie ass cried out as soon as she saw Priest.

"I'm only gone ask you two bitches one time and I promise if I don't get the answers, I'm looking for you will die. Who poisoned my daughter?" Priest calmly asked.

"What the fuck are you asking us for we don't know shit about that?" Jasmine yelled, and Priest let off another shot into her arm. Margie began to cry so hard she looked like she was about to have a nervous damn breakdown.

"Since this bitch wants to die, you got some shit you want to tell us?" I asked Margie.

"I...I'm sorry, it wasn't my idea to hurt that baby. You pissed my daughter off; she's had it out for you for a long time. Keisha is sick; she hasn't been right since she was a kid. She has been in and out of mental institutions most of her life. Diane would always make sure she got her treatments and medicine. When she met you, she made Diane promise not to tell you and mess her relationship with you up. When Diane died, shit spiraled out of control for her. I tried to help her, but she was too far gone and that nigga she with only made matters worse. I knew I shouldn't have gotten caught up in her shit, but the money was just too good to turn down," this bitch said.

"Keisha! You said Keisha was your daughter, how is that possible? I was married to the woman, and I knew her mother Diane," Priest stated.

"No, you knew her foster mama. I'm her biological mama, and Jasmine is her sister. Keisha wanted us to get close to you so that we could take your money and plot to kill your daughter. She has a life insurance policy out on Sasha and was planning to cash in and pay us for helping her. You were doing good, and she was out there struggling. She blew through that money you gave her, and Mazzy helped her spend it. That nigga filled her head up with bullshit, and her dumb ass fell for it. It was Keisha that set y'all up. She knew your brother had drugs in his car because Mazzy told her. It was a few of them in your camp that was in on it. Keisha was messing with this cop, and she called him and told him everything, and that's how y'all got pulled over. I hope you don't think that Keisha was faithful to you because she was fuckin' Mazzy long before she got with you. She was hoping all of you got locked up that night, but you took the rap for it. I'm sorry, I just can't hold it in anymore that shit was eating me up." Margie looked at us. I hope this bitch didn't think because she was trying to be like Usher with these are my confessions bullshit, that she wasn't gone catch these hollow tips.

"Ma, just shut the fuck up!" Jasmine cried. Priest turned to her and sent a bullet right between her damn eyes. Margie screamed as she looked at her daughter's lifeless body.

"Noooooooooo!" Margie shouted.

"Did you put that shit in Zoey's room to make it look like she did it?" Priest looked at her, and she dropped her head.

"I...Oh lord... I swear I didn't want to do that because I liked Ms. Zoey. Jasmine had me put it in her-" She couldn't finish talking because Priest emptied his clip into her chest. Damn, that nigga was mad mad. That old lady was dead when that first shot entered her body. Ion think that was fair. That bitch Jasmine ain't get that many shots. So, I pulled my gun out and emptied my clip in her dead ass. Priest didn't even say shit. He just started spazzing the fuck out.

"Fuckkkkkkkkk! Fuuuccccckkkkkkkkk!" He roared. This nigga was kicking shit over, and I think it just hit him that he made the worst mistake of his fuckin' life. Zoey was innocent. I called the cleanup crew to make sure they took care of this shit.

"We need to find this bitch! I want her dead tonight!" I was with him on that shit, Keisha and Mazzy had to die. I sent a message to Cannon letting him know we need a location on Keisha and Mazzy.

I knew some shit was about to go wrong when they pulled me up to that damn hospital. I was on the phone with my mama when I heard her talking to Nas, and I heard him talking shit to her. At that point, I knew they knew, and Mazzy and I got the hell out of there. Priest calling her back to work, and him telling Jasmine that he missed her was a fuckin' setup. When I first got with Priest, I just knew shit was gone be different for me. My life was rough. I was snatched away from my biological mama and placed in foster care. Margie was a fuck up, and she didn't give a damn about her kids. It wasn't until we all got grown that she decided she wanted to change her life and give a damn about us. I knew she was a money-hungry bitch, and when I went to her and Jasmine about my plans, they were both all in and down to get this money with me. I just knew that shit would work that night I tipped the cop I was fucking off with. We needed them niggas out the way, and Maz would have been able to take over. To most women, Priest was the perfect catch, but I wanted his ass, and other niggas too. I have never been faithful to him, and I didn't feel bad about the shit.

"Maz, you sure your cousin cool with us coming to his house?" I asked him, as we hopped into our rental car. We just got to Atlanta, and this is where we would be staying until shit clears up for us to go back to Philly.

"Yeah, we family. He gone always be cool with me coming. I told you when I called he said to come on down." I hope he was telling the truth because I don't got time for no bullshit. On top of that, we only got five thousand dollars left to our name. When Nas kicked Mazzy out of the crew, that shut shit down for us, and we wasn't able to get no money or drugs from them.

"Ok, I just hope you're right," I told him. It took about thirty minutes to get to his cousin, Randy's house. It was a lot of damn people outside; it looked like they were having a cookout.

"Come on, babe." We got out of the car and walked up on the porch. I must say, these Georgia niggas was fine as hell.

"Maz, what's up, nigga?" Some dude walked up and dapped him up.

"Cuz, it's good to see you, man. This my girl, Keisha. Babe, this my cousin Randy." Mazzy's cousin was one fine ass; I hope my hoe tendencies stay calm while we were down here.

"Hey," I spoke, and he smiled.

"Nice to meet you, Keisha." He winked at me, and my damn pussy jumped.

"Yo, let me introduce y'all to some of my homies. This my homie Denzel, Marlo, Rick, Chad, and my homie Dom. Y'all, this my cousin from Philly, Mazzy, and his girl Keisha," Randy introduced.

We spoke to everybody then Randy led us inside to introduced us to his girl Brandy and her family. Brandy showed us to the room that we were going to be sleeping in.

"Damn, this room small as hell, and why the fuck is it so damn hot?" I complained because this shit was like a damn lil' ass box.

"Look, you gone have to cut that Bougie shit out. They were nice enough to let us stay here."

"You right, I will chill out. Let's go down here and get us a drink and some food. I'm hungry and that BBQ looked good as hell." I knew I had to keep my cool. We went downstairs to get our drink on with his family. The nigga Dom kept staring at me and licking his damn lips. This liquor was making me see things a little clearer, 'cause that nigga could get it. I stood up and walked over to the table to pour me another drink, and when I turned, I smashed right into Dom's chest.

"You good, baby girl?" He licked his lips again, and my pussy was doing a number on me in my fuckin' panties.

"Yeah, I'm good." I smiled and walked back to take a seat next to Maz.

"Babe, I need to make a run to the store." I had a few things I needed to pick up from Walmart.

"Keisha, I been drinking, and these Georgia cops don't play that shit. I will take you in the morning," his drunk ass said.

"He ain't lying. Shit, we all been drinking. What you need, maybe my girl can help you out until tomorrow?" Randy asked.

"Nah, it's personal, and I just need to go to the store." I was getting an attitude, cause Mazzy, and I discussed this shit before we came downstairs.

"I will run you to the store if your man doesn't mind me taking you." Dom looked over at me and then to Maz.

"Nah, you're my cuz homie, I don't mind you taking her. I appreciate that shit but make her ass hurry up. My girl get in a store and she will have yo' ass in there all fuckin' night," Maz laughed and hit me on my ass. I got up and followed Dom to his car. I got in and he pulled off.

"Do I know you from somewhere, you look familiar as hell?" He asked me.

"I thought you look like somebody I knew, but it could be the liquor that got us fucked up," I laughed. When he put his hand on my thigh, I didn't say shit, and he took that as a green light to keep going. I pulled my skirt up and slid my panties off. He rubbed his big ass fingers across my clit, and I lost it. I threw my head back and enjoyed the ride.

"Damn, shawty, you wet as fuck." He pulled his finger away, stuck that shit in his mouth and my ass just started leaking. I slid my fingers on my pussy and started rubbing the fuck out of my shit.

"Mmmmm, shit!" I moaned out, grinding the fuck out of my finger.

"Shit!" He growled and pulled into the back of the shopping plaza, letting his seat back and pulling his big ass dick out. I climbed over into his lap and slid down on his dick.

"Goddamn, ride this dick, bitch!" Dom groaned. I was bouncing on his shit like a porn star.

"Ohhh fuck, this dick good! Fuck me, shit!" I moaned because this nigga was doing a number on my ass.

"Damn, you gone make a nigga cum riding my shit like that," he growled, slapping me on my ass. He gripped my ass cheeks as he guided me up and slamming me down on his dick. That shit sent me over the top, and I was cumming before I could even tell him.

"Mmmmmmm, shit!" I moaned, as my pussy gripped his dick, and I felt his shit pulsating inside of me.

"Fuck!" He growled and shot his load all in my ass. I think I'm gone like it down here in the A, and I'm gone love my new fuck buddy.

Chapter Eleven

KASH

*I*t's been damn near two weeks that I've been here in the hospital. My doctors are saying that I'm healing the way that I'm supposed to and that I may be able to go home in a day or so. Eva has been a great friend through all of this. Ever since I have been out of the coma, she has been here to see me every single day, and I appreciate her because she didn't have to be here. The boys walked into the room, and it was good to see Priest. I know he's been going through some shit, and I understood why he needed a few days to get himself together.

"What's up, man? How are you feeling?" Nas dapped me up and Priest followed.

"I'm feeling good, they said they may let me go home soon." I was ready to get out of here and get into my new home. I didn't even get a chance to move in, because of these bitches. I'm doing everything possible to get better, because I'm coming for every nigga and bitch that came for me. The difference is, I survived; they won't be so fuckin' lucky.

"That's good. I'm glad to know that you're healing. Big Mama told us that you want to go to your house when you get out. I know that she's moving in with me for a while to help watch over Sasha. We thought maybe you would want to come there, that way we can all chip in and help get you better." I knew Priest would want me to be there with them, but I really wanted to be in my own shit.

"I will be alright with y'all coming over to check on me and my mother cooking for me. I should be good to go. It's not like I can't walk, and I know not to overdo it. I'll be fine and if I feel that I'm not...Turn that up." I pointed at the television and we were all sitting here in shock.

"What the hell!" Nas shouted. It was a cosmetic commercial with Zoey in it.

"When did this happen?" I questioned.

"Ion know, but she looked good as hell. I wonder if this is why she moved to New York," Nas stated, and Priest turned to face him so damn quick, I know that shit had to hurt his neck.

"New York! When did she move to New York?" He looked at Nas in confusion.

"Look, all I know is that she and Cas left for New York a couple of days after she came and donated the blood to Sasha. I put somebody on Cas to look out for her, 'cause her ass ain't fucking with me like that right now. I don't know for sure why they're there, but I guess we can kind of put that shit together now. Damn, Zoe, done came up on some real shit." Nas ass was so damn extra. I knew he said that to get under his brother's skin.

"I will be back to see you later, Pop." Priest dapped us up and walked out of the room.

"You ain't shit, you know that," I laughed at Nas, instigating ass.

"That's what his ass gets. Seeing her on television and knowing that she's in New York is going to tear his ass up. I get his first reaction cause that's his daughter, and when he said he found that shit in her room, I'm not gone lie my reaction was the same, but I thought about that shit. I know he's stressed, and I'm gone cut him some slack and help him at least try and see her. 'Cause that nigga needs to apologize, and he needs to do that shit as soon as possible. I'm going up to New York tonight to get Cassie's ass. While I'm there, I'm meeting up with Cam. He said he had some information for us on that nigga, Ronnie. As soon as you're ready, we can put that nigga to sleep. I'm sure that his ass thinks he got the best of you. If it wasn't for you wanting to handle his ass yourself, he would've been a dead nigga right along with his bitch." I know Nas wanted to get this shit over with, and so do I.

"I will be by to see you when I come back." Once Nas walked out, I tried to get up and go to the bathroom, and damn near broke my neck.

"Oh shit, Kash!" Eva yelled as she ran to grab me.

"Fuck. This medicine has me dizzy as hell. Thank you for

helping me, lil lady." I smiled down at her because she still had her arms wrapped around my waist.

"I'm glad I could help you." She smiled. This girl was so fucking fine, and I couldn't help but stare at her. The thought of fucking the shit out of her in this hospital room was driving my ass crazy.

"Ummmm, let me help you into the bathroom. That's where you were trying to go, right?" She looked at me with that sexy ass smile.

"Yeah." Nas was right. Maybe I do need to get to know her better. Once I finished using the bathroom, I opened the door, and she stood to help me back to the bed.

"I see they removed the IV's from you. I'm sorry, I haven't been by in a couple of days, I had some things that I needed to handle for my business. How are you feeling?" She asked.

"I'm feeling good. The doctor said he may let me go home soon. They said I'm healing fine, and I swear I need to get the hell out of here and into my own bed. This shit is driving me crazy. A warm shower and my bed is all that I need." I looked at her and smiled. It seems as if something was bothering her, she looked nervous.

"That's great news," she spoke as she pulled the blankets back over me. Her being this close to me was damn near killing my ass, I couldn't stop my next move if I wanted to. I lifted in the bed and pulled her to me, placing my lips on hers. The moment I pulled her lips into my mouth, and she slid her tongue inside. I wanted to suck and lick every part of her ass. The kiss was so damn good it was almost as if neither of us wanted to pull away. The low moan that just escaped her mouth had me ready to slide inside of this woman and change her fucking life.

"Kash... Ummmm... I shouldn't be doing this. I'm kind of dating someone." She broke the kiss staring at me.

"My bad, beautiful. I don't regret what I did, but I will respect your loyalty to your nigga. I'm attracted to you, and I couldn't hold that shit in anymore. I apologize if I over-stepped my boundaries. What the fuck am I saying, I would do that shit again in a heartbeat. I won't pressure you, though." There was no reason in me lying to her.

"Ohhh...Ummm. Alright, I got you some food, and I need to get back to my office. I will come and check on you tomor-row," she nervously spoke. She turned to walk out, and I had to chuckle.

"You're not going to give me a hug goodbye?" I had to fuck with her. She hugged me every time she left.

"Oh, I'm sorry." She turned, and as soon as her fine ass wrapped her arms around me. I grazed her neck with my tongue, and I could feel her ass shivering in my arms. She jumped away from me so damn quick and ran out of my room. I wanted to invade every fucking thought she has today. I smiled and decided to find something to watch on television.

Chapter Twelve

ZOEY

*I*t's been almost two weeks since I found out that I was eight weeks pregnant. I have cried so many tears since then, and the pain I felt in my heart was unbearable at times. I was having a baby and the father didn't want shit to do with me. I hate the fact that I keep putting myself through bullshit with niggas that treat me like shit. I was scared as hell, that I was pregnant yet again, not knowing if my baby would be alright.

"Zoe, have you decided if you're going to tell Priest?" Cas asked as she sat down on my bed.

"I don't know what I'm going to do. I mean, I know he deserves to know, but that nigga held a gun to my fucking head and put me out. If you guys didn't show up, God knows what would have happened." I still can't believe that shit happened to me.

"I know, sis. I can't believe you have a baby growing inside of you again. I don't want you to worry. This pregnancy is going to be different. I can feel it. Your life is different, and I'm here to help in any way that I can." Just as I was about to respond to Cas, her phone was going off.

"What?" She yelled into the phone and placed it on speaker.

"Bear, why you gotta act like that? I'm sorry shit happened the way it did, but it's time to bring your ass home. I told you I was coming for you in ten days. I was nice enough to give your ass a couple more days. Your time is up, pack yo' shit and come open the door," Nas told her, and Cas went off.

"Nigga, I'm not going nowhere with you and wait. What you mean come open the door? How the fuck you know where we are?" Cas asked him, and I was wondering the same thing.

"I know we were going through some shit, but I don't play when it comes to my girl. I love you, Bear, and I will always have eyes on you. Now come open the door, I'm tired of standing out here." I guess Nas really did come to get her.

"Nah, nigga, it don't work like that. You straight sided with your brother against my cousin. Fuck that! I'm not going nowhere with your ass, and I'm not opening the door." Cas was pissed, pacing back and forth as she hung the phone up and threw it on the bed.

"Cas, don't be like that to him. I understand his position and you should too. To be honest, you took the same position. When it came to me, you took my side instantly. With no questions asked. We can't blame him for taking his brother's side. This is your life, and you both deserve happiness. I'm going to be alright, all I ask is that you keep my pregnancy between us," I said to her. There was this loud ass noise coming from downstairs. I grabbed our gun and tucked it in the back of my jeans. Cas and I ran downstairs, and I couldn't believe what the fuck I just saw. Our damn door handle just hit the floor, and Nas pushed the door open. Both Cas and I were standing here stuck with our damn mouths hanging open.

"Have you lost your fucking mind? You just broke into our shit?!" Cas snapped.

"Technically, this nigga broke into your shit. I just walked in after he was done," This nigga was crazy, but I love how he was with Cas. He had some guy here that took the lock off, and now he was putting the shit back on.

"Zoe, before we go any further, I owe you an apology. I'm sorry shit went down the way it did," Nas stated, I was a little mad, but I can't blame him for standing with his stupid ass brother. I didn't respond; I just nodded. Then I almost fainted when Priest walked through the door.

"Hell nawl! Nigga, you got a lot of nerve bringing your ass up in here. Mmmm, mmmm, nah. You niggas gotta go!" Nas pulled Cas off into the kitchen, and she was still going off. I couldn't believe this nigga had the nerve to bring his ass in here. Everything that happened that night came rushing into my mind. I said that if I ever saw him again, I would never let him know the pain he caused me. And for some reason, I couldn't control the tears. Just seeing him and the flashes of him holding that gun to my head. The hurt and hate that illuminated in his eyes for me that night were so overwhelming.

"Zoe, I'm sorry, baby. I know the shit I did was beyond fucked up, and there is no excuse for treating you the way I did. I know you may not forgive me, but that shit is fucking me up inside. I shouldn't have reacted the way I did without looking into it first. I fucked up, and I don't know how I could ever make this shit up to you, but I will do whatever it takes." I couldn't move, I just stood there and listened to him talk.

"Why are you apologizing? You believed that I did it. You held a gun to my fucking head and put me the fuck out! So, tell me what changed your mind?" I questioned because the more I stood there, the angrier I fucking got.

"I found out that it was Margie, Jasmine, and Keisha that tried to hurt Sasha. Zoe, I know this shit is bad, but you have to know that I'm sorry." I couldn't take this nigga not another fucking minute.

"Sorry, fuck your apology! You fuckin' hurt me! You accused me of trying to kill that little girl. I loved her as if she was my own fuckin daughter. So, no nigga, fuck your apology and fuck you, bitch!" I pulled my gun out and put it to his head.

"Zoe, get that fucking gun out of my face," he gritted.

"Fuck! Zoe put the gun down. You don't want to do some shit you gone regret out of anger," Nas spoke, as he and Cas came running into the living room.

"Well damn, do you, sis. I know somebody we can get to clean this nigga dead bloody ass up when you done," Cas yelled out.

"Zoey, I know that shit hurt you, but you gone have to get that gun out of my fuckin' face." He was pissed. The veins were protruding from the side of his neck, but I didn't give a fuck.

"How the fuck does it feel? You know what? I don't give a fuck how it feels to you. Get the fuck out of my house, and don't fucking come back!" I screamed, and I meant that shit. I was so fucking pissed. My body was shaking, and the tears were falling.

"Zoey, you don't mean...." I pulled the chamber of the gun back and pointed it at him.

"Get the fuck out!" I yelled, and he turned to walk out.

"Nas, I can't do this with you now. I need to make sure she's going to be good before I come back to Philadelphia," Cassie told him.

"Cas, go back and work on your shit with him. I will be just fine. I'm sure you will be back before the next photo-shoot. Don't stop your chance at happiness because of me. Shit happens, and life goes on." I walked upstairs and crawled into my bed, letting all of the pain I was feeling out. I thought that doing the same thing that he did to me would make me feel better, but it didn't. I felt so fucking bad for doing that shit. The look in his eyes and the pain I saw in them, hurt me. It's best that I move on with my life without him. I know at some point I will have to tell him about the baby, but today just wasn't the day.

"Zoe, I think I should stay here with you for a while." Cas walked into my bedroom and sat down beside me.

"Cas, I will be alright. Just go and make shit right with Nas. I will see you in a couple of weeks for the next shoot." I wanted her to leave and fix shit with her man. I loved my cousin being here for me, but I needed this time alone.

"Ok, but just call me if you need me and I will come back." She kissed my cheek and walked out, and I cried myself to sleep.

————

*M*y phone was going off, waking me out of my sleep. Grabbing it off the nightstand, I saw that it was Cas calling me.

"Hello," I answered with sleep still in my voice.

"Hey, boo. I was calling to see if you were ok." I knew she would be worried, but I don't need her to worry about me.

"I'm fine. Did you make up with, Nas?" I asked her.

"We haven't really talked yet, but we will work through it. Thank you for pushing me to give him a chance. I love that man. I was just pissed, but you helped me see his point of view about everything." I'm happy to see that she is willing to work things out with him.

"That's good to hear. Let me get up, I see it's almost eleven, and I need to catch an Uber to the market," I told her.

"Shit, I hate that you're there with no transportation. I will be back up there in a few days, and we can go look for you a car," she stated, and I was good with that because I needed one. Cas and I spoke for a few more minutes, and I ended the call. I got out of bed and suddenly felt sick and ran to the bathroom. Once I got myself together, I stood up and took my clothes off for my shower.

'Good morning, little one. I pray that you remain safe and stay inside of mommy's belly until it's time for you to come out." I rubbed my stomach as I talked to my baby. It took me about an hour to get dressed. Picking up my phone, I ordered my Uber. It took about ten minutes for me to get the market once my Uber came. I don't plan to buy much, but I needed a few things for the next couple of days. I guess when Cas comes back, we will stock up. I'm just tired of eating out; I needed a home-cooked meal.

"Shit just wouldn't sit right with me if I walked out of this store and not tell you how fine you are," A male voice said from behind me. *Damn, he's fine*, I thought. I had too much going on to be thinking about a man right now.

"Thank you." I smiled, and when he smiled, I wanted to melt. He was sexy as hell. His skin was the shade of milk chocolate. His muscles were about to burst through his t-shirt, and he had the most beautiful set of white teeth I've ever seen. He could almost give Priest Chamber a run for his money, but then again, Priest was in a league all by himself. *Urrgghhhh, I had to stop letting this nigga invade my thoughts Like this*. I turned back to look at these damn steaks, 'cause I damn sure couldn't keep looking at his fine ass.

"I know this seems kind of weird, but do you have a man? I want to get to know you, lil' mama. By the way, my name is Tyrese, but my friends call me Ty." Ty held his hand out for me to shake it.

"It's nice to meet you, Ty. No, I don't have a boyfriend, but I'm not looking for anything right now. My life is a little complicated, and I don't want to lead anybody on," I told him. I had to be honest with him. I had to much shit to deal with.

"Well, ain't shit wrong with having a friend, we all need those. What's your name?" he asked.

"Zoey, thanks for the compliment. It was nice to meet you." I smiled and just walked away. By the time I paid for my things at the register, I ordered my Uber and walked outside to wait. It was a nice day in New York, and I'm glad I came out even if it was just for a little while.

"You're sure I can't at least get your number? Wait, are you waiting for someone, do you need a ride? I would never suggest getting in the car with a stranger, but I can't leave you standing out here," Ty stated.

"I'm fine, I have an Uber coming," I told him. The more we stood and talked, the more I wanted to give him my number. I threw caution to the wind, and we exchanged phone numbers.

"You just made a nigga blush. You can't see it from all of this chocolateness, but a nigga damn sure blushing." We both burst out laughing at his humor. My uber pulled up, and Ty helped me put my bags in the car.

"Thanks." I smiled at him.

"I will call you later. Enjoy the rest of your day," he said and closed the door. The driver pulled off, and I asked him to take some detours because you can never be too careful. I didn't want homeboy following me home. I'm not going to get into anything with him, but I guess it would be cool to have a friend in New York.

I felt a little better knowing Zoe was alright. I'm still lying in bed thinking about all the shit that popped off last night. Nas walked out of the bathroom, and all I could do was shake my head. This nigga was fuckin' crazy. I can't believe he hired someone to take the fuckin' lock off the door. A bitch was low key feeling the way he came for my ass. I loved Nas, but I was pissed the fuck off about how my cousin was treated. Zoey put some shit into perspective for me, and I'm so glad she did that. It was damn near four in the morning when we got back to Philadelphia. We both were exhausted and decided to talk about shit later. I mean, we did talk a little on the way home, but I was still showing my ass.

"So, listen up, baby girl. You not gone keep giving me your damn pouty ass attitude. I apologized to you and Zoey. Trust me, I know the shit was fucked up, and believe me, I gave that nigga hell about it. I'm hoping the two of them can work that shit out and get back to each other. I need you to get this shit through your fuckin' head; they shit ain't our shit. I'm not gone lose what I have with you because my brother fucked up. I love you, but check this out. I came for you one time. If you decide to leave and not fuck with me, I won't come for you again." This nigga acts like I told him to come for me the first fuckin' time.

"I didn't ask you to come for me at all!" I jumped up into his face.

"I'm gone need you to bring all that hype shit down a notch. I didn't say you did; I came for you 'cause I need you in my life. I'm just not gone keep chasing you, if you really don't want a nigga chasing you. I don't like all that drama shit. I'm trying to build with yo' feisty ass, not fight with you." He pulled off his shirt, and my damn pussy started jumping around like the bitch was playing double dutch. This nigga knew how I felt when his ass got naked. He was doing the shit on purpose, but a bitch was gone do her best to keep it together.

"I'm going back to New York in a few days. I need to make sure that Zoey is alright. She has a lot of things on her plate, and I need to make sure she stays focused." I needed him to understand that I can't be here with him all the time.

"I'm cool with that. I'm not gone get in the way with what you got going on with your cousin. You just make sure you know where home is, and that's right here with me. Now bring that ass over here, I got a lot of built-up stress to let go." He gave me that sexy ass smile I loved so much. Walking into the bathroom with him, I brushed my damn teeth; I can't be kissing on his ass with bad breath. Pulling my t-shirt and panties off, we stepped into the shower.

"I did miss you. I'm sorry for not being there for you when your dad was shot." I kissed his lips.

"Don't even worry about it. I'm gone beat this pussy up so fuckin' good, you will never make that mistake again." His hands tightly gripped my ass, and that shit made my shit purr. Kissing my lips and sucking my tongue into his mouth caused me to moan out. I have never wanted a man so bad. Normally, I talk shit about his dick but this morning, a bitch gone bust it wide open for his ass. My pussy was deprived, and I needed the dick just like I needed air to breathe. This nigga gone have to just rearrange some shit inside of me, and we gone pray that shit goes back to its rightful place when we're done.

"Shit!" I moaned as he slid his finger inside of my pussy, pulling it out and sucking my juices off.

"I miss the fuck out of you. Don't ever do that shit again, Bear," he spat, lifting me up pinning me against the shower wall and easing me down on his dick. I opened my mouth, but nothing came out, it was like I was stuck.

"Breathe, Bear," he said as he sucked my bottom lip into his mouth.

"Oh fuck! This dick is...Shit!" I screamed as he dug deeper and deeper into my walls.

"Fuck! I need to tear this pussy up, and this shower shit ain't gettin' it for me." He pulled out of me and eased me down. Turning the water off, we stepped out of the shower and went into the bedroom. I crawled onto the bed, was face-down with my ass in the air, and he slammed into my pussy so good I wanted to cry.

"Yeahhh, that's what the fuck I'm talking about. This the type of pussy that will make me kill a nigga," he growled, as he deep stroke every inch my pussy.

"Nasss, I'm cumming! I can't hold it, fuck!" I screamed, gripping the sheets, as he pounded on my pussy like a mad man.

"Come on and give it to me, baby!" He said as he pounded on my spot, pulling all the way out and slamming back into me over and over again.

"Fuckkkk!" He roared, as he came inside of me.

"You do know that I'm not on the pill, and your ass wasn't wearing a condom," I told him.

"I'm in this shit until the end of time. If you get pregnant, that's what it's gone be. We just gone be two crazy niggas with a baby." He shrugged, pulling me up to go take our shower.

"Pop is getting released from the hospital, so I got to go pick him up and get him settled." I know he was happy his dad was doing well.

"Yeah, I got a few things to handle today." About an hour later, we both were headed our separate ways.

Chapter Fourteen

PRIEST

I know I fucked up, but I don't know how I can fix this shit with Zoe. I understand why she is so fucking mad; I'm pissed at myself for the way I did her. I get it, and I take full responsibility for it but shorty tripping if she thinks I'm gone stay away from her. I have never gone down without a fight, and I'm gonna fight because I love her that much. I have been looking for Keisha bitch ass, and even went to the streets on her and Mazzy.

I will stop at nothing to get at her. I can't believe that she tried to take her own daughter out. I'm still fucked up over the fact that I didn't know this bitch like I thought I did. How the fuck you don't tell me some shit like that? It goes to show that her ass was up to some bullshit from the beginning. I can't believe the woman that I thought was her mom, was her foster mom. And to think I was fucking her muthafuckin' sister, this was the craziest shit I ever heard. All over greed and fuckin' money, I put a bounty on Keisha and her nigga. I want them bitches alive. Their death is going to be slow and muthafuckin' painful. If you ever want to pull Priest Chamber back to the streets, fucking with my daughter will get you what you want, quick.

Nas decided to ride back with Cas last night, and I drove his car back. I really need to sit down and talk this shit out with Cassie. She and I were really close, and I hate that this has fucked our relationship up.

"Hey, grandson. Let me fix you some lunch," Big mama spoke, and I picked Sasha up out of her chair. I'm so glad that she was doing better and was able to come home from the hospital. Child protective services ruled us all out after we gave them a recording of Margie's confession. Of course, we had to get our guy to fix that shit up first, but the shit worked. I told the caseworker that I immediately fired Margie. She said that they tried to reach Margie, but they haven't been able to find her.

"I'm good on the lunch. I appreciate you being here with us to help out." I was grateful that she decided to move in with us for a while. I needed to find another nanny for Sasha, and I knew that would take some time. Ms. Carol is due to come back to work today. I decided to only have one cook and have her do the housekeeping as well. I'm paying her double for her duties. It was just best for me to minimize the people that I have working around me and my daughter. I have to make sure that the people I have in my home are trustworthy enough to be here.

"How did things go with Zoey last night?" Big mama asked.

"It didn't, she's pissed, and I can't blame her." I picked up my phone and decided to send Zoey a text.

Me: *Hey beautiful, I love you, and I'm so fuckin' sorry, baby.*

I knew she wouldn't respond, but I wanted her to know that she was on my mind and that I'm truly sorry for what I did to her. I kissed my daughter and grandmother and headed down to my shop. I had a few orders that I needed to finish up. I had to face the fact that I needed to hire a new assistant. I was hoping that Cas would come back to work for me, but I know that won't happen. I walked into my shop and headed back to my office to grab the things I needed for the day. When I'm in the shop alone, I normally work upfront. Turning the music on, and with every move I made, it seems that Zoey invaded my thoughts.

"Fuccckkkkk!" I roared, knocking over the shit that I had sitting on the counter.

"That shit is fucking with you bad, huh?" I turned to see Cas standing there.

"Cas, I know that we should talk, and I really want to talk to you. I don't know if this is a good time to have this conversation." I didn't want this shit to go in the wrong direction with her.

"Nah, nigga, this is the perfect time to have this conversation. You hurt that fucking girl to the core. I'm not gone tell you what you took from her cause you know that shit already. She loved that little girl! No, let me rephrase that shit, she loves that little girl. The same damn woman you accused of poisoning your daughter, is the same woman that saved her life. That shit was all fucked up. I couldn't believe that it was even coming from you!" She yelled.

"She's my fuckin' daughter! How would you feel if you're on the phone with the doctor and he's telling you that, your child was spoon-fed poison?! I wasn't thinking straight. When I found that shit in her closet, it set me off. I fucked up, and I know I fucked up. I love that girl, and I would never hurt her intentionally!" I roared. I was pissed the fuck off. There was no real way to explain my feelings that night.

"Well, bruh, it seems that you got your work cut out for you. Zoey is not gonna come to you easily. She's hurt and mad as hell. Proceed with caution; I can't help you get her back. I will be back and forth from Philly to New York. I'm not sure that I will still be able to work for you and manage Zoey's career. If I can't help you, I will find a replacement for you," she stated and walked out. Everything she said was true, I have to figure a way to get Zoey back. Sasha is always calling out for her mama. I'm just not sure if she will ever come back to us now.

Chapter Fifteen

NAS

Getting back right with Cas had to happen, I wasn't taking no for an answer with her ass. Like I told her, the shit my brother and Zoe are going through is fucked up, but that's their shit, not ours. I'm gone always ride for my brother, but if he wrong about some shit, I'm gone tell his ass he wrong. As soon as I had time to think about that shit, I knew in my heart that nigga had it all wrong. We will always support and be there for them, but I refuse to let that shit come between me and my girl. When my pop got shot, I went through some shit, and I needed Cas. We had already lost our mom, and losing Pop would have been catastrophic to this family. I was out West with Cannon. We had a shipment that came in and I needed to make sure shit was good with that.

"Did Cam get you the information you needed?" Cannon asked.

"Yeah, we good to go. We know exactly where that nigga lay his head, and where all his spots are. We're just waiting on Pop to get his shit together. He wants to be there, so he halted our moves. You know I hate waiting. When shit pop off you supposed to handle that shit right then. You can't let these niggas think shit sweet," I said to him.

"I feel you, but you know your Pop was the coldest nigga in the game, and his moves are always on point. I know it's gone be some shit when Big Kash lay that murder game down and my ass gone be right there with him." Cannon was right, my pop was no joke when it comes to killing a nigga. They fucked up when they came for him, and I can't wait to see what the fuck he has in store for this nigga.

"Yeah, you right. I will let you know when we ready to move on them niggas. Did you get any word on that nigga Mazzy and his bitch yet?" I asked him.

"Nah, but best believe niggas is looking for their ass. Ever since Priest called and put that bounty on their head. Them niggas can't step foot back in Philly without us knowing about it. Wherever they are, they better stay tucked, because your brother is out for blood," he stated. Priest was a nigga that played no games, and it took a lot to bring that nigga back to the streets. I think he was more ruthless than Pop and I put together.

"Yeah, it's definitely going to be a blood bath. Let me get out of here. I need to go check on Pop. He just came home from the hospital today, and I want to make sure he's good." I dapped Cannon up and left out. Cas was calling, and I picked up, on my car speaker.

"What's up, my beautiful Bear?"

"Babe, what time are you coming home?" She asked, and I knew her ass wanted me to do something.

"I should be there in a couple of hours, why?" I questioned.

"I need you to stop by Priest's house. Big mama told me that Ms. Carol made some damn Lobster mac & cheese and porterhouse steaks," she laughed.

"Bruh, you might as well meet me over there 'cause ain't no damn way I'mma make it home with that shit in my car. I will be on the side of the road in my car fuckin' that food up. I will call you when I'm leaving Pop's house, and you can meet me there," I told her.

"Ummmm, I don't know if Priest wants me over there. I kind of cursed him out earlier." I knew that shit was coming, but she better grow some damn girl balls 'cause a nigga ain't gone stop me from eating.

"You was bad enough to curse his ass out, be on yo' gangsta shit and walk up in that nigga house and eat his food. 'Cause a nigga like me gone eat his shit and talk shit to his ass if he got something to say about it." We both burst out laughing.

"Just call me when you on your way." Cas was a damn trip, but I loved her feisty ass. We ended the call, and I pulled into Pop's driveway and headed into the house. He gave Priest, and

I keys to use because it was going to be too much for him to get up and down.

"Pop!" I called out to him and headed upstairs to his room.

"Hey, son. What's up with you?" He asked, sitting up in the bed.

"I just wanted to make sure you were good. Did Priest come by after I dropped you off?" I asked him.

"Yeah, he brought me some dinner," he stated.

"I'm about to go over there and grab me something to eat. I got all the shit I need on yo' boy. I see the security posted up outside the crib." Priest and I decided to get our men over here. Because Pop wasn't in no shape to be fighting off a nigga right now.

"That's good. I should be ready in a couple of weeks to handle that shit." Pop didn't seem like himself and I wondered if he really was ok.

"Pop, you sure you good?" I looked over at him.

"Yeah, I'm good, just want to get this shit over with." I understood where he was coming from.

"I feel you on that. I just came by to check on you real quick. I will be by to see you tomorrow. I love you, Pop." I dapped him up and walked out. I called Cas and told her that I was on my way to Priest's crib, and by the time I got there, her car was already in the driveway. Walking into the kitchen, Cas, and Big mama was sitting at the table.

"Where is Priest?" I asked.

"He's in his room. He doesn't do much talking these days.

That boy is stressed out and mad at the world. I guess he has a lot on him with the shit that's going on with Keisha, your dad, Zoey, and Sasha. It's a lot, and I feel for him, but he gone have to make shit right with Zoey." Big mama shook her head.

"Ma, she doesn't want shit to do with him right now. I think he gone have to let her come to him. He apologized, what more can he do if she doesn't let him?" I asked them because I was confused about that part.

"He gone have to put them damn knee pads on and do a little groveling." She shrugged.

"I will apologize for my fuck up, but a nigga ain't crawling and begging yo' ass to forgive me over and over again. Nah, I don't have that many fucks to give if I got to beg you like that. I can tell you how I'm feeling, and admit to my wrongdoing, but that's it, boss," I told them.

"Babe, you know you were begging me to come back to you last night," Cas laughed.

"Yo' ass was dreaming the shit happened that way. I told you to bring your ass on and how I felt about you. I love you, and I missed yo' fine ass, so I came and got you," I said to her, and fixed me a damn plate. Cas ass was already sucking on her damn fingers. We sat around and talked our shit for a little while, before heading home.

Chapter Sixteen

KASH

A **month later**

*W*e were sitting outside of Ronnie's crib, watching him pull out of his driveway heading to his meet with his crew. Now that his ass was gone, It was the perfect time to pay his bitch a visit. We had someone in his camp that gave Cam all the information on this nigga. It's amazing how money will get a nigga to turn on you in a heart-beat. I have been waiting for a long time to get my revenge on these bitches and the time was here. Nas, Cannon, Cam, Priest, and Dame were here with me to make sure shit goes smooth.

"Let's go," I spoke as I got out of the truck with both of my guns in hand.

"Alright, Nas, Cannon and I are going to the back and get into the house. If the alarm is on, I will disarm it, and we will let y'all in," Cam spoke, as he and the guys walked off. It took about ten minutes for them to open the front door, and we walked into the house. The guys moved around to check the house, while Priest, Dame, and I went upstairs. Once we cleared the top level, I opened the door to the master bedroom. My dick instantly got hard at the thought of killing this bitch. Walking into the bedroom, I could hear the shower going. I decided to take a seat in the chair that was in the corner of the room, while Priest searched the room. Placing my guns on the table, I pulled my Cuban cigar out, lighting it up and waited.

"Who this nigga think he is, Al Capone?" I heard Nas whisper to the guys as they stepped into the room. We heard the shower turn off, and a few minutes later, she walked out of the bathroom.

"Babe... Ohhhh fuck! No...No...Nooo! Kash, wha...How did you get in here?" She nervously asked as she ran to the nightstand next to her bed.

"It's not there, bitch! You just gone run for your gun thinking we would even let you pull that piece of shit. It's a room full of niggas with guns in here, you dumb bitch! You set me up for your nigga, coming up in my shit with that sob ass fuckin' story." I put my cigar out and walked over to her as she pleaded for her life. Gripping her ass up by the neck and slamming her against the wall.

"I'm sorry he made me do it. I really liked you, but shit was just too complicated!" She cried.

"Bitch, fuck you!" I threw her on the bed and emptied my clip in that hoe ass bitch.

"Yooo, we got company," Cam yelled. Everyone pulled their guns out and got in place.

"Stormy!" Ronnie yelled out. A few seconds later, he came running into the room and saw his dead bitch in the middle of their bed.

"Nahhh, man, fuckkkkkkk!" He roared, just as gunshots sounded off out in the hallway. As soon as he turned to go help his men, it was too late. We had the drop on his ass. I stepped out and Priest let off a shot into his ass, and Ronnie started shooting wildly around the room. I sent a shot into his body, and his gun hit the floor. Just as he tried to grab it, Priest kicked it out the way and pushed his ass to the floor.

"You think this shit is over, nigga! You a dead nigga!" He yelled, and I kicked him in his bitch ass face.

"I have been waiting for this day. You actually saved me a trip to your lil fuckin' meeting. I can almost figure out how you knew we were here for your bitch. Pulling out my machete, I sliced the side of his face.

"Fuckkkkkkkkkkk!" He screamed out, as he tried to swing on me. Priest sent another shot into his body, and I smiled at my ruthless ass son. He was itching to send that fatal shot, but he knew this shit was personal.

"The only niggas that's gone die in here tonight is you and your crew." I slammed my machete down on his neck severing his head from his body. I got tired of looking at his bitch ass and was ready to get my ass out of here.

"Box that nigga head up, and hand that shit to his friend," I spoke.

"Pop, I know you pissed, but how we gone hand that shit to his fuckin' friend? We don't know who this pussy hang with. Do you got that nigga's address?" Nas crazy ass asked.

"Fuck!" Dame spat, walking into the room and froze seeing Ronnie's body lying on the floor headless. Priest picked his head up off the floor, swung it at Dame, and the nigga jumped out of the way.

"What the fuck!" Dame yelled.

"Yeah, that's the same shit I said when I realized it was you that shot me. That's the reason your bitch ass didn't come to visit me that much while I was in the hospital. We were supposed to be boys! You were my fuckin' brother! I always wondered why you were still cool with this nigga when you knew I couldn't stand his ass. When I woke up in that hospital, shit slowly started coming back to me. At first, I was like nahhhh, not my nigga. I put Cannon up on game and the shit we found out was fucked up. We didn't meet that nigga by chance, you knew who he was. I know all about your friendship. Y'all played me good all these fuckin' years! Ronnie may have called the shots, but bitch, you pulled the trigga on my ass. Nigga, you were going to try and set me and my sons up, so you and this pussy nigga could take over our shit!

"What?!" Nas put his gun to Dame's head.

"You always had the best of everything, you had to be that

nigga. All the women wanted you; you even took the one girl that I wanted more than anything. You knew I liked her, but yet you swooped in, and the next thing I know y'all together and getting married and shit."

"Careful, my nigga. Bringing up my mother will get your ass bodied before you can take your next breath!" Priest told him.

"Pop, you saying this nigga set you up?" Nas asked.

"Nigga, you commented that my wife was fine when we first saw her. It's not my fuckin' fault you didn't make your move. You're a delusional ass nigga, but get this shit, don't speak on her again! This nigga is the reason they knew we were here. I'm surprised they weren't waiting on our asses to come through the door, but he wanted me to kill Stormy. He couldn't stand her ass because she chose Ronnie over him, and she gave me the pussy. Ohhhh, you didn't think I knew about that shit, huh? Technology and good muthafuckin' people on your team is some shit every nigga in the street needs. I wish I would have had that same mindset years ago, but I would have never figured that it would be you," Pulling my gun out, I sent two shots to that nigga head killing him instantly. Cam had his cleanup crew come in and clean this shit up, but I had made such a mess they were planning on torching it once they got the bodies out.

"Damn, that's fucked up, I can't believe that nigga Dame was a snake ass nigga. Pop, why you didn't tell me that shit?" Nas asked.

"I didn't tell you because you would have gone after him. I

know you; I had to get all the information and do this shit my way," I told him.

"I guess you right about that shit." We were headed back to Philadelphia. I need a hot shower, my medicine, and bed. I was healing, but I still had a little pain here and there.

———

Waking up the next morning, Eva flashed through my mind. I haven't heard shit from her, I didn't know my lil move on her was gone stop her from coming to see me. I needed her to know how bad I wanted her ass. I know I didn't make the best decision with that bitch, Stormy. However, there is definitely something about Eva that has touched the core of me. The only other woman that has done that was my wife. So, I don't think I'm giving up on Ms. Eva so fast. I guess I will give her time to get herself together, and then I'm coming for her ass and I won't be playing fair. I decided to go downstairs and make myself some lunch. My phone was going off. When I looked to see who it was a smile spread across my face.

"Hellooo," I sang into the phone.

"Pop, it's your move. You left me hanging last night, and the game was getting good. I think you intentionally didn't want to move because your ass was about to lose." I burst out laughing at her antics.

"Zoey, it was late, and I fell asleep. These damn pain meds has a way of taking my ass out," I said to her, and we burst out laughing. I put her on speaker and made my move in online backgammon. I knew that my mom had her contact information, and I wanted to talk to her about what happened. I understood her pain and hoped that one day she would forgive my son. She made me promise not to tell him that I was in touch with her, just as she made my mother promise her, and I had to keep my word. That shit was killing my boy; it was written all over his ass. I knew what type of man Priest was, and Zoey better watch out, because I know damn well he's not letting her go.

"Yeah, yeah! Wait, ohhhh my God, I didn't see that move. I just knew I had you; you get on my last nerve," she pouted.

"My name is Kash, baby. You better ask about me." I laughed, just as my doorbell sounded off.

"Zoe, let me call you later, someone is at the door." We said our goodbyes and I got up to go answer the door. I was shocked to see her standing there, but welcomed her in.

"How are you feeling?" Eva questioned.

"I'm better, how have you been?" I asked her, as I leaned against the wall taking her in. She seemed nervous, and the shit was sexy as hell seeing her like that. I didn't want her to be nervous around me though.

"I was just about to make me something to eat, you want to join me?" I asked.

"No, thank you. I ate this morning," I chuckled, and I knew for sure her ass was nervous off of that crazy ass response.

"So, what you're saying is because you ate this morning,

you don't do lunch? It's almost one in the afternoon, come sit and have a bite to eat with me. All that damn food you were bringing me while I was in the hospital, you can at least eat a damn burger with me," I laughed, grabbing her hand, pulling her into the kitchen.

"Why don't you sit and let me cook it for you?" she said to me, and I pulled a seat out for her to sit.

"Nah. I got this, beautiful lady." I poured her a glass of wine, and I went to prepare the burgers. It took me about thirty minutes to get the food cooked, and I fixed her plate and sat it down in front of her.

"Thank you." She smiled.

"Why did it take you so long to come and see me?" I asked her, as I stood in front of her. The shit was on my mind, and I had to know what was going through hers.

"Kash, I think you know why I haven't been by," she said to me.

"Hmmmm, stop running from me, and shit won't be so hard. You're dating him, is he your man?" I asked, pulling her up from her seat.

"No, but I wanted to give him a fair chance at this because we've discussed making things official," she spoke.

"Fuck that. This game ain't fair, baby. Are you fucking him?" I traced her jawline with my fingers, and her breathing became a little more erratic.

"Once," she answered truthfully.

"Hmmmmm, don't fuck him again. Do you want to know what I think? I think your lips need to be kissed, your mind needs to be assured, your body needs to be touched, and your fuckin' pussy needs to be savagely deep stroked. And the only person that you truly want to do that for you, is me. Open up and let me in, baby, and I will take care of all that shit for you," I whispered in her ear, as I kissed the nape of her neck.

"Ohhh...Ummm." She couldn't even get her words out.

"But I meant what the fuck I said, don't let that nigga touch you again." She shivered, and I walked away with a smirk on my face. Grabbing my plate and as soon as I walked back to the table, she stood up.

"I think I need to go," she nervously spoke.

"Nah, I don't think you need to leave. I think you could do one or two things, sit and let's eat these burgers or lay and let me lick, suck, and eat on you." She just stood there, not saying shit.

Fuck it. I pulled her into me, crashing my lips onto hers. The way our tongues collided and wrapped around one another had me ready to suck the soul out of her ass. I was hungry for this woman, and nothing, not a muthafuckin' thing was going to stop me from having her today. She was going to be mine for the next twenty-four hours. If I had anything to do with it, I'm going to etch my name into her body with every fuckin' deep stroke I give her. Every time she walks, her pussy gone be screaming for me. Only wanting me inside of it. Pulling her upstairs with me to my bedroom, I began removing her clothes. Seeing her wrap her arms around her, as if she were trying to cover her body pissed me off a little.

"There is nothing wrong with you, move your fucking

arms so I can see all of you. Be confident in who you are. You're fuckin' beautiful, and I'm gone have fun sucking every part of you." And I did just that, starting from her lips all the way down to the treasure between her legs.

"Kash, ahhhhhh!" she moaned, as I began swirling my tongue on her pearl and then latching onto it. I could feel her pussy pulsating inside my mouth, and that only drove me to go harder.

"Your pussy taste so fucking good," I growled out, spreading her legs further apart and gripping her ass, as I feasted until she started screaming my name.

"Kashas, I'm... ohhhh shit! I'm cumming!" She screamed, and I kept going because I wasn't finished. I wanted to pull all the juices out of her. I'm gone send her back to that nigga empty.

"I taste it. Give me some more of it, baby." I slid my tongue inside of her and went off on this pussy.

"Fuck, suck that shit! Ahhh, this shit is so fuckin' good!" She moaned as she gyrated her pussy harder into my face. This muthafucka was juicy, and I have never enjoyed eating pussy as much as I'm doing right now. I felt her pussy pulsating, and her thick ass legs began to put me in a chokehold. I knew she was about to cum again.

"Mmmmmm, fuckk!" She screamed, and I sucked her pussy dry. I stood wiping my face, as I pulled the rest of my clothes off, grabbing a condom from my drawer and sliding it on. Pulling her to the edge of the bed, I rubbed my dick up and down her slit, entering her with ease. A single tear fell from her eye as I stroked the hell out of her. All you could hear was the sounds of our lovemaking.

"What the hell, Pop! Ohhhhhh, hey stepmamaaaa!" I heard Nas ass at my door, but I didn't give two fucks about him being there. He needed to get the fuck away from my door, and out of my fuckin house.

"Kash!" Eva cried out, as I deep stroked her walls, and her body began to shake. Neither of us could speak, we just let that shit go as we both released together.

"Baby girl, I'm not letting this pussy go. You gone have to gone and let that nigga know what it is." I smiled at her and pulled her into the bathroom.

"I can't believe we got caught." She held her hands to her face.

"Eva, we're too damn old to get caught. We're grown as hell and free to do what the fuck we want. Especially up in here, that nigga just got an ear full of some good shit." I smacked her on her ass, and we got into the shower. The power of the pussy is a muthafucka. I licked, sucked, and made love to her ass into the wee hours of the morning. I think I overdid it, but it was all worth every bit of pain I was feeling.

One month later

For the last couple of months, I have been working, and my baby was growing. I was four and a half months pregnant, and I swear I looked every bit of five or six months. I know that I should have told Priest about me being pregnant, but as time went on and I put shit into perspective, the more I thought about it, the angrier I got with his ass. I have been going to the doctors, and he told me that the baby is developing fine. I have had two new contracts since I did Blu. I did a shoot with Gucci a couple of months back, and I just did one with a maternity magazine. Things between Ty and I were cool. He turned out to be a nice guy. He's in the streets, but I actually enjoy spending time with him. We haven't taken it there, because I'm not gonna be disrespectful while I'm carrying another man's baby. Ty knows that I'm in a complicated situation, and he's being respectful. He's a nigga from the streets, and I know damn well he's not waiting on me to have a baby to give him some pussy. I have gone on a few dates with him, but again, it's only been a couple of months. I just celebrated my birthday a few days ago, and he took me out to dinner. Cas was trying to come up and I told her I really didn't want to celebrate my birthday. I received all types of gifts from, Priest, and I haven't opened any of them yet. Ty and I were sitting here eating pizza and Ty picked up the remote to turn the TV on.

"What you want to watch, ma?" He asked.

"Whatever you choose," I said, sitting down next to him. When the commercial of me from Blu came on, he looked at the TV then over to me. I was eating my pizza like I didn't see his ass staring at me.

"Zoe, stop eating that damn pizza. You know damn well I'm trying to figure out why yo' fine, beautiful ass is all over this damn television." I burst out laughing because the look on his face was funny as hell.

"Okkkk, I'm a model as you can see." I smiled.

"Why the hell didn't you tell me?" He asked.

"I don't know. I told you I'm here on business. I guess I just didn't want your reasonings for wanting to be my friend to be for the wrong intentions. I mean, we're still getting to know each other, and it would have eventually come up." I shrugged.

"I get it, but check this out. I don't need your money; I got plenty of that shit. I'm not the type of nigga that's gone ask you for a dime. I know we just met, but I'm not one of these bum ass niggas trying to eat off his girl. I tried to get you to spend some time with me in my world, but you always insist that I come here." He sounded offended and that wasn't my intention.

"I apologize, if I offended you that wasn't my intentions," I told him.

"We're good, just let me know when you really want to get to know me," he said, and I just nodded. I feel like our whole night was messed up because he didn't say much after that. I heard the door open, and I had no clue Cas was coming up tonight. I kind of kept Ty a secret, and when she comes up, I kept him away. Oh well, I guess I have to tell her about him now.

"Zoe! Ohhh, ummmm....Hello," she spoke with this goofy-ass look on her face.

"What's up?" Ty spoke.

"Ty, this is my cousin, Cassie. Cas this is my friend, Ty. Why didn't you tell me you were coming in today?" I asked her.

"I thought I would surprise you, but damn, I'm the one surprised." She giggled.

"Ty, give me a minute. I will be right back," I said to him, as I followed Cas upstairs to her room.

"Girl, who in the fine fuck is that nigga down there?" Cas asked me with this amused look on her face.

"I met him a couple of months ago, but we're just friends, Cas," I said to her.

"Chile, I couldn't just be friends with that nigga, lawd. Did you at least let him lick the twat? I know your ass about ready to climb the walls to dickville by now," she stated, and damn was she right. There were some nights I wanted to pick up the phone and call Priest just to come and fuck me. I knew if I did that, I would have to talk to him, and I didn't want to talk to his ass right now. Every day since the night he showed up with Nas, he sends a text message saying that he's sorry. And every Friday morning, I get two dozen of yellow and white roses delivered from him, and the cards always say how sorry he is.

"You're right, but I'm pregnant, and I can't sleep with another man carrying Priest's baby. That would be so fucking trifling of me." I sighed.

"Biiihhhh, that nigga would be wrapping that tongue around my shit every chance I could get. The tongue ain't gone touch the baby. Well, wait, I guess that depends on how long that nigga tongue is. Girl, don't listen to me. That's my hoe shit trying to come up out of me. I guess I understand where you're coming from. Ummmm, ma'am, when the hell do you plan on telling Priest about the baby?" She looked at me.

"Soon. I plan on coming to Philly in a couple of weeks and I will talk to him then," I told her.

"Zoe, the maternity magazine drops in a few days, what if he sees it?" Cassie was worried for no reason.

"Cas, it's a maternity magazine, he would never see something like that. He has no reason to even have a maternity magazine," I said to her. I was damn near nude on the cover, but it was tasteful, and the shots were so beautiful of me and my baby bump.

"Ok, if you say so. I'm leaving to go back to Philly tomorrow night. The family is getting together for dinner at Priest's house, and I promised Nas I would be back for it." I have been going through it not seeing Sasha. When Cas is over there, she would facetime me so that I can see her pretty little face.

"Ok, I guess I need to go back to my guest. We will talk when he leaves," I told her.

"Zoe, what the hell is this?" She asked.

"What do you mean, it's a check for the work you've done. Please don't mention that check I gave you a couple of months back, that was payment on the Blu deal. We've had two more deals since then and I've made a lot of money. That two hundred and fifty thousand dollars is yours, and you earned every bit of it." I smiled and left her standing there with her mouth agape.

"You good?" Ty asked, looking up at me.

"Yeah, everything is cool. I just didn't know she was coming in tonight." I smiled and took my seat next to him.

"I'mma get out of here and let you spend time with your cousin. Hit me tomorrow when you have some free time, and maybe we can grab some dinner," he said as he kissed my cheek, and I pulled his face back for a kiss. He stared at me for a moment, as he pulled my lips into his mouth. The kiss was so damn good, and my pussy was ready to do flips on his ass. He picked me up, and I wrapped my legs around his waist, as our kiss deepened. I don't think my baby was feeling this, it felt like he or she were doing backflips in my belly.

"I think we should chill before you have dick all up and through your ass. I can't play these types of games, ma." He put me down.

"I'm sorry," I said to him.

"No need to apologize. I will talk to you tomorrow." He kissed my cheek and left out. That was pretty intense, and I'm not sure if I want to take it there with Ty. I need to definitely clear the air with Priest before I make any drastic decisions with another man.

Chapter Eighteen

PRIEST

One Week Later

I was just getting back from Atlanta. My new store opened up this past weekend. I have a deal to open more stores in Las Vegas, Miami, and Cali. The business side of my life was definitely doing some big things, but the shit with Zoey was not good at all. She won't even talk to me. For months I have been apologizing and asking her to just talk to me, and she never responds. I know I deserve the shit, but at the same time, that shit was pissing me off. I think it was definitely time for me to pay her another visit, and if she pulls a gun on me, then that's just what, lil mama gone have to do. I miss her ass like crazy, and my baby girl is always calling for her. It's almost like she sees her every day. I would have thought that Sash would calm down about her, but she hasn't. Walking into the kitchen, Nas, Cas, Tiff, and Big mama was eating dinner.

"Is that all that you guys do, come here just to eat my shit? I can understand my grandmother; I would feed her without a doubt. I bet if I didn't have Ms. Carol, I wouldn't see none of y'all asses as much." I told them as I fixed my plate.

"Nigga, share the wealth!" Nas dumb ass spoke, and they all burst out laughing.

"I know that's right. You don't have to act like that. I've been beating these hoes up for you since I was in my mama belly. I remember when I heard her cursing at yo' ass when she was pregnant with me, I drop kicked her in the bladder for you. The least you can do is let me eat for free," Tiff crazy ass said. We all looked at her and burst out laughing.

"Nigga, what?! Tiff, yo' ass was reaching with that shit. You kicked her ass so hard she pissed herself, huh?" Nas was laughing so damn hard he was hanging off the chair.

"Y'all some damn clowns, I swear. Cas, how is Zoey doing? I saw her Gucci commercial; her career seems to be taking off." I looked over at her.

"Yeah, she's a hot commodity these days. Zoey is doing good, and having the time of her life," she stated.

"I'm so proud of Ms. Zoey. I saw her on the cover of this magazine while I was in the grocery store this morning. She's so beautiful with her baby bump, and I know she's going to make a wonderful mother," Ms. Carol said, pulling a magazine out of her purse.

"Baby!" We all yelled at the same damn time, and Cas was stuffing her face so much she started choking. Nas jumped up and grabbed the magazine from Ms. Carol.

"Yoooooo, she pregnant for real. Cas, why the fuck you didn't tell us she was pregnant?" Nas asked her.

"Listen, that's not my business. That's her business to tell." Cassie shrugged, just as Nas passed the magazine to me. My body felt like it was going to shut the fuck down. Her ass was lying on the floor with some sheer shit draped across her breast and pussy, with the most beautiful round pregnant belly I have ever seen on a woman.

"Cas, is this my baby?!" I asked her mad as hell.

"I can't talk to you about Zoey's business. That's something you will have to ask her, but you need to proceed with caution fuckin' with my cousin," she said. I could feel the heat rise in my body. My ass needed some answers, and I picked up my phone, trying to call her ass, but she kept sending me to voicemail.

"Nah, she not gone ignore my ass today. Either that's my damn baby, or she started fucking the day she got to New York." I called her phone again, and she still didn't pick up. Jumping up, I ran upstairs and packed me an overnight bag.

"Bro, where are you going?" Nas asked.

"I'm going to New York. Big mama, I will be back in a couple of days," I told her.

"Priest!" Cas yelled out, but I kept going. I waited until I was about thirty minutes away from her address, and I called Cam.

"Priest, what's good, bro?" He asked, picking up on the first ring.

"Hey, man. I need to get inside a crib, can you meet me there? I'mma send you the address," I asked him.

"Yeah, you know I got you on that shit. Do I need to bring some other tools with me?" He asked.

"Nah, I'm good. I just need to get inside if she doesn't let me in. I'm sending the address to you now, meet me there in thirty." This is a game that Zoey's ass don't want to play with me. I will fuck you up over my damn kids, and if that's my baby she's carrying, I know I'm gone lose my muthafuckin' mind. When I pulled up, Cam was already there, and I was happy as hell. I dapped him up and walked up the stairs to ring the doorbell. I waited a few minutes and rang the bell again, but it still was no answer.

"Give me a few minutes. She has a keypad on the door, but I got something for that," Cam stated. I'm glad these niggas knew how to get into people shit without damaging some shit. The night I came with Nas, Cam couldn't come, so he sent a nigga to take the lock off the door. Cas was ready beat his ass, and Zoey was literally ready to shoot a nigga. That's exactly what she was gone have to do tonight!

Cam came back, sprayed some shit on the keypad, and placed this plastic piece over the pad.

A few seconds later, five prints appeared on the plastic. Cam played with the numbers on the pad for a few seconds that the prints showed up on and the fuckin' door unlocked. This shit was crazy, and I'm damn sure gone have to upgrade my systems at home so this shit won't happen to me. He did the same thing to the alarm and was able to disarm it quickly.

Once I was situated in the house, Cam left out. I sat on the couch waiting for her to come home. It was a little after ten and her ass wasn't home. I heard the door open and hearing her voice, along with a male voice, had my ass on edge. I know damn well this chick don't have a nigga with her! I pulled my gun, sat it in my lap and waited.

"I'mma go make our plates and you go get comfortable," I heard the dude tell her, and my ass was ready to erupt.

"Thanks, Ty." When I heard them kissing, that shit did it for me.

"You might want to get your pregnant ass in here and get the fuck away from that nigga!" I roared, still sitting in the same spot. They both appeared in the living room, and this bitch ass nigga had his gun drawn on me.

"Who the fuck are you, nigga?" He asked, and I looked over at Zoe.

"It's best that you get this pussy out of here. This is some shit I don't think you want to get involved with, my nigga," I calmly spoke.

"Priest, how the fuck did you get in here?" She asked me.

"You really gone ask me some shit like that? I guess my question to you is, did you forget to tell me something? Or is it that nigga's baby in your stomach?" I asked her, and she dropped her head, looking at the floor.

"Priest," she called out.

"Answer me!" I yelled.

"Nah, nigga, you not gone talk to mine like that," this nigga said, walking further into the living room.

"Ty, I got this. Let me handle this. I'll call you later. I will be alright," Zoey said to him, and that nigga still didn't budge.

"Nah, this nigga acting like he that muthafuckin' nigga. Let him be that nigga." This clown ass nigga was still talking shit, and I stood up walking up to them.

"Bruh, this is not a game or a muthafuckin' test. This is not what you want, I promise you. Shit gone get bad for you real quick," I told him.

"Nigga, fuck you, and your pussy ass..." I didn't give him time to say shit else. I crashed my gun down on his face, knocking his gun out of his hand and beat the shit out of his bitch ass. He was throwing them hands, but he was no match for the shit I had to get off of my chest.

"Priest! Please stop!" Zoey screamed, and I continued stomping this nigga the fuck out. I drug his bitch ass to the door and beat his ass down the steps. I don't know who the fuck they thought I was, but I guess it was time for Zoey to see who she was really fuckin' with. I tried practicing being the new and improved Priest Chamber, but it was always some shit that will bring the old me out. I was on one tonight, and I wasn't playing no fuckin' games with her or this bitch made nigga.

"Who the fuck is that nigga?" I asked Zoey as I pulled her back into the house and left his bitch ass on the sidewalk.

"He's a friend, and you didn't have to do that shit to him," she cried.

"You better not shed another tear over that nigga. Talking that shit like I won't put a bullet in his muthafuckin' head!" I was so pissed I wanted to go back outside and light that pussy nigga up.

"You don't get to break in my shit!" She yelled, walking up on me.

"Fuck all that shit. So you with that nigga? Is that his baby or is it my baby?" I looked at her waiting on her to answer me.

"Yes, it's your baby. I haven't slept with anyone else. I was going to talk to you about it, but I was gonna do it on my time." I swear this girl almost made me call her some shit I knew I would regret later.

"When the fuck were you going to tell me, Zoey?" I asked her. I couldn't believe this shit. I know I fucked up, but she can't play no games like that with me. I left her standing there and walked outside to get my bags, her bitch ass nigga was gone. I walked back into the house, and her eyes grew wider.

"Where the hell are you going with that?" She questioned.

"I'm gone be right the fuck here with you for a couple of days. We got a lot of shit to talk about. Oh, and you might as well dead that shit with your nigga. If that's my baby inside of you... Nahhhh, I'm not doing none of that shit. Set up and emergency visit with your doctor first thing in the morning. I want to see my baby, and get caught up the progress of your pregnancy," I told her. I'm not gone have no other nigga laid up with her ass, rubbing his hands over her damn stomach, while my baby is inside of her. Fuck that!

"We are not together!" She yelled at me.

"That's cool; I know what the deal is with us. Now come sit and talk to me about my baby." I was so pissed, and I was doing my best to calm down, but that shit was hard as fuck to do right now. I sent a text to Cam. I needed to get some information on this nigga she been spending time with. I also needed to put a man on her, so that I knew where she was at all times. The playing field is different now that I know she's carrying my seed.

———

The next morning, I heard Zoey moving around in her room. I was sleeping in the bedroom next to hers, and I climbed out of bed to handle my hygiene. Once I was done, I went to her bedroom door. I started to knock but changed my mind and opened the door. She was standing there with her beautiful naked body on display, and she jumped at the sight of me.

"You should knock before coming into my room," she said with attitude.

"I didn't want to knock." I walked up to her placing my hand on her stomach. She tried to move back, but I pulled her closer to me.

"I get that you're pissed, but I'm gonna want to touch your stomach. I've seen your body and been inside of you, countless times. I have never seen your body with a life that I helped create inside of you, don't take this moment away from me. I think you did enough of that since you're halfway through your pregnancy," I said to her as I bent down to kiss her belly and turn to walk out of the room. When I made it back into the room, my phone was ringing.

"Yeah."

"Bro, I wanted to make sure everything is cool. I heard Cas on the phone talking to Zoey. So, you had to beat a nigga ass last night, huh?" Nas questioned.

"Yeah, the nigga was just doing too much shit-talking for me. She said the baby is mine, so I'm going to spend some time up here with her. I need you to do me a favor, can you and Cas bring Sasha up here tomorrow?" I asked him. I know that it's been a while since the two of them have been together. They deserve to see each other, and I want to make that happen.

"Yeah, I got you. Take it easy on her, and congratulations to you both," Nas said to me and we ended the call. I went to take my shower, and when I got out, Zoe was standing in the room. I dropped the towel from my waist, and she started fidgeting with her hands.

"You need something?" I asked her with a smirk.

"The doctor can see me; we need to be there in an hour," she stated.

"I will be dressed in a few minutes." She turned so damn quick she almost bumped into the damn wall. I knew this shit wasn't going to be easy, and I didn't expect it to be, but we were going to have to figure this shit out.

$\mathcal{I}$ almost flatlined when Ms. Carol started talking about Zoey being pregnant and pulling the damn magazine out. When Priest left, I snuck off to the bathroom and tried to call Zoey, but the heifer phone was going straight to voicemail. Nas and I argued all damn night about that shit because he felt like I should have told him. He said that was some shit that his brother needed to know about. I agree that Priest needed to know, it just wasn't my place to tell his ass. I finally got in touch with Zoe this morning, and she told me what happened. I was hoping that she wasn't with Ty, but she told me that nigga got his ass handed to him. We just pulled in front of Zoey's house in New York because Priest wanted us to bring Sasha up here.

"Let's make this quick, I have to be at the club tonight,"

Nas stated as we got out the car and grabbed Sasha and her bags.

"Yeah, Tiff and I are supposed to come to the club tonight," I told him. Walking into the house, Priest was coming down the stairs smiling when he saw his daughter. Sasha was jumping and giggling at the sight of her dad.

"How are things going with Zoe?" I asked him.

"It's going, we. We went to the doctors yesterday, had conversations about the baby but that's about it. It is what it is, she's pregnant with. She has my baby inside of her, and the fact that she's been hanging with that nigga has me pissed. So, we just gone be pissed together for a lil' while. Nas, did you go by the shop and get the things I asked for?" He questioned.

"Yeah, it's in my trunk. I will get them out in a minute," Nas stated. Zoey came walking downstairs down the stairs, and when she noticed Sasha, the tears instantly came, and Sasha damn near jumped out of her dad's arms.

"Ma-ma, ma-ma." Priest put Sasha on the floor, and she took off running to Zoe. When Zoey grabbed her up into her arms, I swear I wanted to cry seeing. Seeing them together like that was the sweetest shit I have ever seen in my life. Zoey didn't speak; she just turned and walked back upstairs with Sasha in her arms.

"Damn, that shit almost made my thug ass shed a tear." I laughed at my crazy ass man, but I felt where the hell he was coming from.

"I'm going to go check on them," I said and walking off. I

went into Zoe's bedroom she was playing and laughing with Sash.

"Thank you, I never expected to see her here," she spoke. I'm so glad that Priest did this for her.

"This wasn't our doing, Priest called and asked that we bring her up here. I'm just glad that you two are together again. How are things going with y'all since he's been here?" I asked her.

"Cas, I'm still trying to grasp that he's here. I get an instant attitude when I see him. I feel so bad that I didn't tell him about the baby. You should have seen him at the doctor's appointment yesterday. He had so many questions. We both decided that we didn't want to know what the sex of the baby was. I'm just praying that everything goes well with my pregnancy. I'm almost five months, and I have never made it this far with any pregnancy, so I'm excited about that," she stated. Sasha stood up in the bed kissing and Zoey on her cheek.

"Awww, she is so sweet. I'm happy that you get this time to spend with her, try to relax a little. The stress is not good for the baby, I know you're upset with Priest, but maybe you should at least come to some common ground with him. You two are having this baby, and for the sake of your child, you both have to make peace. I'm not saying you have to be with him, I'm just saying you need to be able to co-parent. You don't have anything else planned until after you have the baby. So, this is the perfect time for you to get your life back on track. I talked to Mom last night, and I'm so glad you told her." I smiled at her.

"Yeah, she's been calling and checking on me. I told her she should come to visit, and she said she was going to wait until the baby comes." I knew my mom was going to be excited about Zoey having a baby. She's been pressuring me about giving her a grandbaby.

"Well, let me go we. We have to get back, so Nas can get to the club. Wish you were going to be there with us. Me and Tiff crazy ass are hanging at the club tonight." I shook my head because I knew we were going to have a good time.

"Girl, she called me this morning talking shit about me not telling her I was pregnant. I know Big mama, and Kash are going to be upset. I'm going to call them and apologize, and I hope they forgive me." Zoey shrugged. I gave her and Sash a hug and went back downstairs.

"Everything good?" Nas asked me.

"Yeah, they're so happy to see each other. Sasha is up there kissing on Zoe's face; it's the cutest thing I've ever seen. Priest, I know shit is tough right now, but take care of her. You're gonna have to fight for her, if you love her enough to do that," I told him, Nas dapped his brother up, and we left heading back to Philly.

———

*L*ater that night, I pulled up to the valet at the club, gave them my keys, and walked inside to get my drink on. *Hot by Young Thug ft. Gunna* was blasting through the speakers as I made my way to VIP. For some reason, I felt like eyes were on me, but I kept it moving. Tiff and her friend she said she was bringing with her were already sitting at the bar.

"What up, sis?" Tiff got up and gave me a hug.

"Hey, sis," I spoke.

"Yo, Janelle, this my sis, Cas. Cas, this is my homegirl Janelle," Tiff introduced, and Janelle looked familiar, but I couldn't figure out where I knew her from.

"It's nice meeting you, Janelle," I said to her, and took a seat. *Juicy by Doja Cat & Tyga* came on and that got my ass going.

"Bartender, give us another round, please!" Janelle yelled over the music. She passed Tiff her drink and then passed me one, and we were getting fucked up. I should have eaten before I left home because these damn drinks were hittinhittin' my ass hard, and I was feeling good as hell. Nas walked up to me; my damn man was fine ass fuck tonight.

"Sup, you good?" He asked me.

"Yep, I'm cool, daddy, just. Just feeling real good right now." I stood up wrapping my arms around him, kissing his lips.

"Alright, be easy on the drinks. I just wanted to check on you, I got this party going and I need to make sure shit good with that," he said to me.

"Yo, bro, this my friend, Janelle. J, this is my bro, Nas; he owns the club," Tiff introduced them.

"How you doing, this? This is a nice club," Janelle said to Nas, and he nodded.

"Preciate that, y'all. Y'all have fun. Yo, Dana, drinks are on the house for them," he said to the bartender. He kissed my lips and headed back to handle his business.

"Damn, they're partying they ass off down on the first level. Let's go down there and fuck some shit up," Janelle yelled out, and we all downed our drinks, leaving the VIP and heading downstairs to the dance floor. I have never partied down here before; it. It was a little crowded, but it was cool. When *Dior* by Pop Smoke ft. Gunna came blasting through the speakers, we were on one.

"I'll be right back, I got to gotta go to the bathroom," I told Tiff, and she nodded. Just as soon as I reached the bathroom, someone grabbed me and pushed me up against the wall. It was kind of dark, and for a second, I thought it was, Nas and I wrapped my arms around his neck. When I focused and saw who it was, my ass was fuckin' shook.

"What's up, baby, it's? It's been a minute. Why the fuck do you think it's safe to run from me, Cas? The city big, but it's not that fuckin' big. I knew I would eventually find your ass," Black said, kissing my lips, as he tried to slide his tongue in my mouth. I got my bearings and tried to get away from him, but shit got bad real quick. Black was being slammed to the floor, and Nas was fuckin' his ass up. Security came and pulled him off of Black, and they pulled Black out of the club.

"Bitch! You in my shit, kissing on another nigga! I will kill your ass up in here. "

"Nas, baby, listen to me. I wasn't doing shit. That was Black…" He cut me off by gripping me up.

"So, you see your ex nigga, and gone disrespect me in my shit! I thought you were a real one, bitch, you. You ain't shit but a fuckin' hoe. Feeding me that bullshit about his bitch ass, but yet you all wrapped up with the nigga in my shit! Get the fuck out of my muthafuckin' club, before I fuck yoyo' ass up," he gritted, just as Tiff ran up.

"Bruh, what's going on?" She asked him.

"I just caught this bitch with some nigga tongue down her muthafuckin' throat," He yelled, and Tiff looked at me, shaking her head.

"Damn, Cas, what the fuck!" Tiff looked at me, disappointed.

"It wasn't like that," I cried, trying to explain, but Tiff walked off. Janelle was standing there with a smirk on her face, and the next thing she did had my ass in an uproar.

"You good, daddy?" She asked Nas, rubbing her hands on his chest.

"Bitch!" I screamed and punched that bitch dead in her shit. She started swinging on me, and I tried to beat that bitch head in.

Nas lifted her up into his arms and carried her away.

"Nas! Nassss!!" I tried to go after him, but security escorted me out of the club. A few minutes later, they pulled my car up, and I could barely get myself together. Once I was able to drive, I went home and waited for him to get there. I can't believe how shit got fucked up so damn fast. I was heartbroken that he treated me like that. I know the shit looked bad, but it wasn't what it looked like. I'm scared out of my mind that I ran into that nigga. I hope and prayed that he wasn't lurking and followed me home. I crawled into bed and cried. I wasn't going no damn where until I talked to Nas. A few hours later, I heard the alarm beep, and he came walking into the bedroom.

"Yo, shorty, I'mma need you to leave my shit. I'm not gone put my hands on you, but you foul as fuck, and you gotta go," he snapped.

"Nas, he pushed me against the wall! I wasn't kissing him; he just kissed me," I cried.

"Bitch, your arms were wrapped around that nigga's neck, I saw the whole thing. When he grabbed you, I was on my way to beat his ass. Until I saw you wrap your arms around that nigga, I slowed down just to fuckin' watch you two niggas. Your ass wasn't fighting that nigga off, that's. That's what females do when a nigga fuckin' with them, that ain't they nigga. They beat the shit out of his bitch ass for touching them. You didn't do none of that shit. Nahhh, I'm not listening to none of that shit you talking!" He yelled and walked out, slamming the door, and I just cried. He was so pissed and hurt, that shit just ripped my heart to pieces. Even though I was hurt, I didn't want him feeling like that. The longer I sat there, the angrier I became because we were supposed to be better than that. We promised each other that we wouldn't jump to conclusions, that we would talk shit out first. I got out of bed and walked out of the room in search of his ass.

"I don't give a fuck how mad you are. I'm not going no

muthafuckin' where! I didn't kiss that nigga, and if you call me another bitch or hoe, I swear I'm gone fuck yoyo' ass up in here. I know it looks bad, but that nigga pushed me against the wall and kissed me. I was in shock because, at first, I thought it was you. In my mind, only my man would be pulling on me and pushing me up against a wall. I was drunk and I'm still a little fucked up. For some reason, I felt a little more fucked than I would usually get off of four drinks. I'mma let you have this shit tonight because I know how bad this shit looks.

You can be mad, and we don't have to talk, but I'm not leaving my muthafuckin' house. If I find out that you did anything with that lil' bitch you helped and got cozy with tonight, I'mma make sure I get at yoyo' ass and then I'm coming for her. You niggas kill me with that shit, y'all can fuck up a thousand muthafuckin times and expect us to forgive you. If a nigga even thinks his girl fucked up one time, that shit will shut a nigga's whole damn body down. I did nothing wrong and I'm not going to sit here and let you treat me like I the fuck did! One more thing, you better find this nigga, because something is up with him." I was so fucking mad I was shaking. I went back to our bedroom and broke down. I hated to show my emotions in front of a nigga, it made you look weak, but I could only take so much of this shit. I love that man, and I be damn if I'm just gone sit and let him think I would do some fucked up shit like that to him.

Chapter Twenty
KEISHA

Shit with me and Dom is heating up. I been riding that nigga dick just about every day. He had to stop coming around so much because he was getting too damn attached, and Maz was noticing the way he was acting with me. That shit caused so many damn arguments with Maz and I. I'm not gone lie, I was loving it here in Atlanta, and I was damn sure feeling Dom fine ass. He picked me up a couple of days ago, and I haven't been back to Maz's cousin's house since. I was lying in his bed, and just thinking about him had my ass hot and bothered. He was in the bathroom taking a shower, and I was lying there naked waiting on him. I needed to get this nut out of me, so I slid my fingers over my pussy and began rubbing my clit. That shit was feeling so good I started to grind harder against my fingers. My eyes were closed, I was so into it I didn't notice Dom come out of the bathroom. I just felt his hands spread my legs apart and him sliding that long-ass tongue up and down my pussy.

"You just gone fuck on this good pussy and leave me the fuck out," he spoke between licks.

"Mmmm, hmmm, shhhhhit," I groaned. The way he was licking and sucking on my shit, a bitch was ready to cum all in this nigga mouth. He moved my hand out the way and was sucking the hell out of this pussy.

"Ahhhhhh fuck! I'm about to cum!" I groaned, as he replaced his tongue with his dick and fucked the hell out of me. Pounding into me so damn hard, I was damn near running from the dick.

"Fuck this! This pussy got a nigga ready to bust!" He growled, and a few minutes later, we both were cumming.

"Damn, you keep fuckin' a nigga like that you gone have to leave that nigga you came down here with." He was right; I was ready to leave Mazzy ass the fuck alone. I had a better time fucking with Dom, and I was feeling his ass heavy.

"Babe, you got a t-shirt?" I asked him.

"Yeah, go look in my top drawer on the left," he said as he walked into the bathroom. Looking in his drawer, something caught my eye as I grabbed the shirt. It was a picture, and I knew this chick. When it hit me, I ran into the bathroom.

"Who is this girl to you?" I asked him, holding the picture up.

"That's my ex, why?" He questioned, looking at me like I was crazy.

"She's with my ex-husband, she. She lives up in Philly now," I asked just to be clear.

"Yeah, I saw her some months ago, and she was in a club with my cousins Priest, and Nas. Them two niggas live up in Philadelphia, you need to tell me what you know," he said to me.

"Your cousins! Priest is my ex-husband, and this chick is his girl," I told him.

"Damnnn, that's why you looked familiar to me. I saw you with him on some pictures at my mom's crib. I got something for that nigga though, they. They jumped me in the club that night over this bitch!" Dom was pissed. A thought hit me, and a smile spread across my face.

"That nigga took my daughter and won't let me see her. He got this bitch raisin' my child, but he gone get his. I'm gone see to that shit." I started crying to add some emotion to my bullshit. Knowing that this nigga had it out for Priest only made shit better for me. Mazzy ass acts like he was lil' scared of they ass, but Dom seemed like he was about that life.

"Stop all that crying. I'mma get that nigga and you gonna get your daughter back. I know that nigga eating up there too, so we gone get that bread as well. I'm already planning to hit his shit he done setup down here," he said.

"You promise you gone help me get her back?" I question, as I wiped my eyes.

"I got you, baby, but you gone have to leave that nigga. I want you over here with me in my shit every night. If I have to go over there and get yo' shit, that's what the fuck I'm gone do, he. He a pussy looking ass nigga anyway. The fuck he let his girl leave the house with a nigga like me? I'm telling yoyo' ass now. I'm not that nigga to fuck with, so if you gone be my girl, you better act like you fucking know. As a matter of fact, we going to get yo' shit when we get dressed." He pulled me into him, kissing my lips.

Damn, I just knew it was about to be some shit with Mazzy. If Dom can help me get at Priest ass, I'm with it. I know he did something to my mama and sister, 'cause I had been calling them and they asses weren't picking up. It took us a couple of hours to get dressed, and we were just pulling up in front of Mazzy's cousin's house.

"That nigga and his cousin can talk all the shit they want, but I know Randy is a bitch. Let's get this shit over with, so we can go grab us something to eat. A nigga starving, and I might even take you to meet my mama with yoyo' fine ass." Dom pulled me in for a kiss, and we got out of the car. Walking inside of the house, Mazzy was sitting on the couch, smoking weed and talking to Randy.

"Where the fuck you been, Keisha?" He asked, jumping up from the couch.

"I been around, I just came to pick up my shit. I'm moving in with my man. I'm sorry, Maz; shit just ain't working out for us," I said to him, and this nigga had the nerve to charge at me. Dom punched the shit out of him, and he hit the floor.

"Yo, Dom, what the fuck you doing, that's! That's my

cousin nigga. How you gone just fuck his girl like that, that's? That's some foul ass shit." Randy was going off, but that shit didn't faze me or Dom.

"Nigga, do it look like I give a fuck about yo' fuckin' cousin, she? She don't want his ass no more! Keisha, hurry up and get your shit," Dom said to me, and I walked upstairs to grab my bags. When I made it back downstairs, Mazzy was going the fuck off, but he wouldn't come near Dom. He was calling me all kinds of hoes and bitches.

"Let's get the fuck out of here," Dom said, as he bent down and slid his tongue inside my mouth right in front of Mazzy. That nigga was about to lose his mind, and I thought that was the funniest shit ever. He was gone be pissed when he goes upstairs to see that I took the rest of the money. We stopped and picked up some dinner and decided to chill for the rest of the night.

"Babe, you want to watch a movie?" I asked him.

"Yeah, we can do that, I haven't watched television in so long. My ass don't be home long enough," he laughed. I turned the television on and got the shock of my life.

"Dom! Look at this shit," I told him, and we both just stared at the screen.

"The fuck! This bitch is working for Gucci. This is what my mom was talking about, she. She said that she saw this bitch on TV. I brushed the shit off, so this is how this bitch is living, huh?" He seemed bothered, and I felt a little jealous of his reaction. I got up and walked out of the room, because I didn't want to say shit that would set him off. We have already gotten into a lil' argument a couple days ago about some shit that was so fuckin' petty to me. I had a feeling that he still loves that bitch, Zoey. So, I'm wondering if he saw her, what would he really do to her.

"Why you walk off?" He asked, walking into the bedroom.

"I just wanted to lay down, that's all. Do you still love your ex?" I had to ask him, 'cause that shit would drive me crazy if I didn't.

"Nah, not really, she. She did too much shit for me to go back to her ass. The only person I want is you, baby, let's. Let's focus on that."

Chapter Twenty-One

NAS

I was on fuckin' fire about the shit that happened at the club. I was walking out to talk to my security to let them know that we were at capacity and not to let anybody else in the club. When I saw Cas and that nigga hugged up and kissing, I wanted to kill that nigga and fuck her ass up. I fucked up because I was supposed to look for that nigga months ago and handle his ass. I heard what the fuck she said, but I was too muthafuckin' pissed to go sleep beside her ass last night. Walking into the kitchen, she was making breakfast, and I grabbed something to drink and walked out. Just thinking about last night, had my ass pissed all over again. I was so fuckin' pissed I went back downstairs and gripped her ass up.

"If I find out you on some foul shit, I swear I will kill your ass," I told her, and I meant what the fuck I said.

"And if I find out that you fucked that bitch, I'm gone kill yo' muthafuckin' ass. I told you what happened, why would I go through all the trouble of getting away from him, just to get back with him? That shit don't make no sense, and you know it don't," she spoke. I stared at her for a minute and left the kitchen. I went to take a shower, so I could hit the street. I didn't fuck Tiff's friend, but it came damn close. And that was a first for me. Normally, I would've had her ass bent the hell over. Once I got out of the shower, Cas was sitting on the bed. Not saying shit to her, I walked into my closet to find something to wear for today.

"So, this is how you gone leave shit? You just gone threaten me, and then walk off. I didn't do anything fuckin' wrong, and I'm not gone let you just treat me like I the fuck did! That shit ain't cool. I love every bit of you!" She cried. Hearing her cry was fucking with me, I was a sucker for her ass. Even though I was pissed, I had to put my shit to the side.

"Stop crying, that shit just had me in my feelings, but we're good." I kissed her lips, and she pulled away.

"You telling me to get out of your shit did something to me. I thought when I moved in with you, that this became our home. I felt like I was stripped down to nothing, I mean, I have money, but it had me feeling fucked up. I gave up my place to come here with you and to know that you can just say fuck it, get out my shit, just ain't the move for me. To be honest, that shit made me feel uncomfortable as fuck. I love you, and I will go to war for you and with you, but I can't be

feeling like that. I have to know that I'm secure in my relationship and my fuckin' home," she said, looking at me, and I
saw the hurt in her eyes.

"I'm sorry, babe, that. That shit wasn't cool, and it won't
happen again. I said we were gone do this relationship shit
differently, and I spazzed out on you last night. I don't want
you to feel uncomfortable, so I will fix that shit. Just know
that I'm gone get at that nigga, he. He fucked up coming in
my muthafuckin' shit, fuckin' with mine." This nigga may not
know who I am, but his pussy ass about to find out.

"I think you should look into that bitch, Janelle. Something is up with that hoe, and I need to know what it is," Cas
stated.

"I will look into her ass, now. Now come here and let me
show you how sorry I am." Pulling her shirt over her head, she
didn't have on a bra. I licked my tongue around her nipple,
sucking into my mouth as I played with her pussy.

"Your shit always wet for a nigga," I said to her.

"Always. I need you to fuck the shit out of me, Nasir," she
moaned as she grindgrinded her pussy against my fingers,
trying to get her shit off.

"I got you, baby." Pulling her to the bed, I never missed a
beat, massaging her pussy. I sat down, as she crawled on top,
easing down on my dick. Cas was a beautiful ass woman, and
the way she was throwing this pussy on me was different. It
was as if she was trying to prove a point.

"Damn girl, ride this shit!" I gritted, biting down on my
lip, stroking the fuck out of her. She eased up to the tip of my

dick and slammed back down on me, grinding and gyrating her pussy on me. That shit had my toes digging in the carpet. If I wasn't careful, I might break one of them muthafuckas. Gripping her ass cheeks and spreading them apart as she pressed her body against mine and bounced that pussy up and down my shit, had a nigga ready to let all this cum loose in her ass.

"Fuck this! This dick is so fucking good, I'm about to cream all on your shit," she spoke, and I lifted her up fucking the shit out of her ass.

"You love this dick?" I flipped her ass over and gave her this work.

"Ohhh, fuck! Yesss, fuck me! Fuck the shit out of me!" She screamed, throwing her pussy back, and I did just that. I fucked this girl so damn good; she was talking in tongues. For a split second, I thought the damn devil had shown up.

"God damn! Fuckkkkkkk," I roared, filling her ass up with cum. I think me and Bear just went half on a baby.

Chapter Twenty-Two
KASH

I was still fucked up knowing that a nigga that was supposed to be my brother, turned on me. This game is a muthafucka and it's hard to find loyal niggas. I'm glad that shit is behind us, and we can move on. I spoke to my mom this morning, and she told me what was going on with Zoey and Priest. I picked up my phone to call her. I'm glad she didn't tell me that secret because there was no way that I could keep that information from my son.

"I'm sorry, please don't be mad at me," Is the first thing she said.

"I'm not mad, baby girl. I'm kind of glad you didn't tell me, especially if you wanted it to remain a secret. That's something that you shouldn't have kept from him, Zoe. I get that you two are going through some shit right now, but you should have told him." I can understand if she didn't tell him right away, but to be halfway through her pregnancy, is a different story.

"I know, he's here with me now. He's upset about it, but we're working through it," Sheshe spoke.

"That's good to know, so do you know if you're giving me a grandson or a granddaughter?" I asked her.

"No, we've decided to wait and let it be a surprise we. We will be grateful with whatever God blesses us with." I could hear the happiness in her voice.

"I'm with that, he or she will be loved no matter what. Well, call me later, and we will start a new game. I'm ready to beat that ass again," I laughed.

"You wish, I'm gonna win this time," she laughed. I beat her in every damn game.

"I don't think so, but a girl can dream if she wants to," we both laughed, and ended the call. Eva came walking out of the bathroom, and I just smiled. Shit with her and I were going good. We haven't made things official. We wanted to get to know each other and take things slow. It was like we connected on a deeper level, and I loved it. I couldn't get enough of her, I damn near lived inside of her ass. She told me that she talked with ole boy, and he didn't take the news well. All I know is that nigga better act like he knows when it comes to fuckin' with her.

"Hey, beautiful." I smiled as she crawled in bed and kissed my lips.

"Hey, baby." She smiled, as she laid her head on my chest.

"As much as I want to stay in this house, and between

them thighs, I have a surprise for you, so. So let's get dressed and get out of here. It took us about an hour to get ourselves together, and we left out. I pulled up in front of Bianca's and we got out of the car. It was a Saturday night, which is one of the busiest nights for my business. I decided to close it down for the night and do something special for Eva.

"Kashas! You did this for me? Oh my God, this is beautiful. I love yo... I love it." I had to chuckle because baby girl was about to let that shit out.

"I'm glad you love it." I pulled her seat out for her and waited on the chef I hired to come and serve us. I had my jazz band come in and play some music for us while we ate dinner. The entire scene was romantic. I wanted her to get use to this shit because this is the type of man that I am. I believe in showing my woman how much she means to me. Being with Eva is refreshing, and the start of something beautiful.

"I can't believe you did all of this for me, look. Look at all of these roses and candles. I pulled out a gift and sat on the table, pushing it in front of her.

"I know that we've been spending a lot of time together, and I'm loving every second of it. You're beautiful, your heart is pure, and your desire to be who you are unapologetically, that shit is sexy as hell to me. Eva, I will never tell you that I'm a perfect man. What I will tell you is that when I wake up each morning, my thoughts are about you. I loved my wife more than anything in this world, and she gave me my children. I know that in order for me to move on, I have to allow my heart to be open to something new. And being with you is allowing me to do that. I'm not gone rush you but know that I want you to be mine," I told her, and she opened the box.

"This necklace is beautiful, thank. Thank you, baby. Just so you know, I don't want to be anywhere else but with you," she said, and I stood to pull her up into my arms. I wanted so bad to make love to my woman right here in this damn restaurant, but I remembered that I did that shit with Stormy. I wanted to create new memories with Eva. After dinner, I decided to go take a walk down on Penn's landing with her and it was a beautiful night to do it.

"I love being out like this with you. I'm so ready to go home and fuck you to sleep." As soon as the words left her mouth, I scooped her ass up and walked back to the car. I'm always ready to slide in the pussy, but I've made it a point to show her that it was so much more than just fucking her. I cared for this woman, and I feel like the more time I spend with her, the more my feelings evolve for her. It took us about thirty minutes to get home, and I swear we could barely make it in the house. The fuckin' party started in the car when she gave me some of the best damn head of my fuckin life. I almost fucked a few cars up trying to get here. We were stripping our clothes off before we could even get into the house good. I was kissing and sucking on her ass like she was the last fuckin' meal I was gone get in this lifetime.

"Kash!" She whimpered.

"I'm right here, baby," I said to her as I sat on the couch, and she crawled her fine ass on top of me, easing down on my dick.

"God damn! Where the fuck have you been all my life! This is my fuckin' dick, and if you give it to another bitch, I'mma kill you and that hoe," she groaned, as she rocked her body back and forth.

"Fuck! We're doing it like that, huh? I hear you lil, lil' mama, talk yo. Talk yo' shit while you ride this dick." I was almost caught off guard with her lil' threat. I said that same shit to my wife. I knew other niggas said that shit to their girls, but I never heard a woman say that shit to me. I see my baby coming out of that conservative shell and giving me that gutta shit inside of her ass and I loved all that good shit.

"Ohhh God, this dick is so fucking good. Baby, fuck me from behind, and I want you to fuck the shit out of me." I gave her exactly what she was looking for. I thrust into her ass so hard I heard sounds I ain't never heard before from her fine ass. I pulled my dick out and slammed back into her again.

"Damn, this pussy good as fuck!" I growled, as I deep stroked her shit.

"I'm cumm... On God, I'm cumming, shittttttt!" She screamed, and I swear she was pulling the cum right out of my ass to the point that a nigga was seeing stars. What the fuck!

Chapter Twenty-Three

ZOEY

It's been a few days, and Priest and Sasha are still here. Shit with us has been tense as hell, but I love that Sash is here with us. She eases the thoughts of me wanting to kick his ass out, out of my mind. I feel so bad about my friendship with Ty. I have been calling him, but he won't answer my calls. I know he's mad at me, and I'm praying that he doesn't start no shit with Priest. Ty was wrong for saying that I was his. I never gave him any indication that we were together.

We actually talked about not getting in a relationship. I mean, we were attracted to each other, and if my ass wasn't pregnant, I know for a fact we would have been fucking. We've even kissed, but that still doesn't mean that I'm his girl. I had just given Sasha her bath and put her to bed. I wanted to get comfortable, so I decided to take my shower. Priest was downstairs working on a few pieces that he had to finish. I guess this is the life of owning your own shit; you can do it from anywhere. He was making it hard to stay mad at him, even. Even though we're in the same house, he stills sends me a text message every morning apologizing. Once I was finished with my shower, I walked out into my bedroom and jumped because he was leaning against the wall.

"You scared the shit out of me! I'm pregnant, you can't do that," I told him.

"I'm sorry. I wanted to come and check on you, so I decided to wait until you got out the shower," he said to me.

I grabbed my robe to put it on, but he walked over to it and took it out of my hand.

"What are you doing?" I asked him, reaching for my robe.

"I want to see you naked carrying my baby, you. You have no idea how fuckin' beautiful that is. Don't you miss me, baby? Because I miss the fuck out of you. I miss touching you. I miss everything about you. I know this shit is my fault, but I would give anything to wrap my tongue around your pussy right now. I would give anything to plant myself deep inside of your walls and feel your pussy grip my dick like only you can. There is no woman that can do that for me, Zoey. Just imagine it, imagine my tongue working its way inside of your pussy. Imagine me latching on to your clit and sucking that muthafucka until you scream my name. Fuck, I want to hear you scream my name. I want to see the faces you make when I'm deep inside stroking your pussy over and over again. Don't you want to feel good?" He asked me, and I swear I was on the verge of cumming just by him talking to me. This nigga was good, my breathing became rapid as he slid his finger across my lips.

"Priest," I whispered.

"You want me to touch you, you. You want me to lick you, suck you, and I know damn well you want me to fuck you. It's been a minute for both of us; my dick is throbbing so bad for you to the point that this muthafucka pains me," he said to me. I was standing here damn near shaking from the thought, and my pussy was so damn wet, I had to clench my thighs together. He got closer to me and I couldn't move.

"I need to taste you, I need to feel you, all I want to do is make you cum," I swear I did just that. I was cumming it was oozing out of me and down my thighs. I can't believe this nigga made me cum and his ass didn't touch me.

"Fuck!" he snapped, picking me up and placing me on the bed. I couldn't even stop him if I wanted to. I was too far gone, and I needed him. He moved his tongue in a circular motion around my clit, and that caused my body to quiver. As he sucked and pulled it into his mouth, I was losing my mind. My stomach was doing flips, and it wasn't because of the baby. I could feel the explosion building up inside of me.

"Priest...I can't take it oh! Oh my God. I can't hold itttt, fuck!" My body was shaking. I could barely breathe as the force of my orgasm shot through me. I have never came so hard in my life. Priest was still licking and sucking the juices out of me.

"I'm gonna fuck the shit out of you, do. Do you know how

hard it's been for me being in this house with you and not be able to touch you?" He gritted, as he got behind me, raising one of my legs and easing inside of me. I couldn't move I was stuck. The strokes he was giving me was deep and oh so fuckin' good.

"Fuck this pussy is so fuckin' good! I love the fuck out of you, Zoey. I'm so sorry, baby. I'm so fuckin' sorry, I need you to forgive me," he spoke, and I couldn't respond because I was too emotional. The way his dick caressed my pussy was on another level that only he could take me.

"Ahhhh shit! I'm cumminnng!" I screamed, there. There was no way that I could hold it in. This nigga was doing a number on my ass, and he was pounding the fuck out of me.

"God damn! Fuck!" He growled, as he hit my spot over and over. I was cumming yet again, and this time he was releasing with me. We both were just lying there in our own thoughts, trying to catch our breath.

"Priest, I know that you're sorry, and I understand that we have a lot of things to work through. Just because we had sex doesn't fix the issues we have. You hurt me, and you hurt me badly. I'm not in a place where I'm just gonna run back to you. Yes, I love you, and the lovemaking was beautiful. However, just because we fucked, that's not going to make me jump. We need to work on building our friendship and trust for one another back to the way it was. Can we start there?" I asked, looking over at him.

"We can do whatever it's gone take to get you back in my life, but I'm not gone raise my kids in separate homes. I will give you time to get your thoughts together; I just hope you get it together by the time you have our baby. I'm going back to Philadelphia tomorrow, Zoey, you. You need to end whatever you have with this nigga. If he tries me again, I'm going to kill his ass. You just keep that in mind when you're calling him trying to apologize," he spoke, getting out of the bed and leaving the room. Damn, I had no idea that he overheard me leaving Ty a voicemail. I don't want to start more drama between Priest and me, but I did enjoy having Ty as a friend. I damn sure don't want to see him dead, because of me.

Chapter Twenty-Four

KEISHA

Shit with Dom and I have been going good. I'm loving every minute of being here with him. Thank God I don't have to pretend that I like being in that tiny ass box they called a house anymore. Mazzy has been calling my damn phone, leaving voicemails nonstop cursing my ass out. I don't give a damn about how he feels, I need somebody that's going to help me get what I want. For couple of weeks now, I've been asking him when we were going back to Philadelphia, and he kept saying he thinks we should stay down here and leave shit alone. The nigga was weak, and now he wanted to fuck up the plan. How the fuck was we supposed to live off this lil' bit of money we had left. I heard Dom coming in the house, he. He walked into the living room and sat down beside me.

"What's up, you cook dinner?" He asked.

"I sure did, your plate is in the microwave. Did you get everything set up for us to leave?" I questioned, following behind him to the kitchen.

"Yep, we leave tomorrow," he spoke. We heard a crashing noise, and Dom pulled his gun out.

"The fuck was that?" He asked, walking out of the kitchen. I followed behind him to see what the hell was going on. Dom and I went towards the back to check everything out and we found nothing.

"It must have come from outside," he said, just as the doorbell sounded off. Dom went to the door and swung it open, and I swear this nigga has to be the dumbest nigga I know.

"Nigga, you must want to fucking die coming to my shit," Dom snapped on his ass.

"Fuck all that. I need to talk to my girl!" This nigga was crazier than my ass. I'm not his fuckin' girl.

"Mazzy, what the fuck are you doing? I'm not your girl, I'm with Dom and you need to fucking leave!" I yelled.

"Nigga, you need to listen to her before I beat that ass again," Dom told him.

"Keisha, you need to get your shit and come on, all. All these years we been together, and you gone just leave me over a clown ass nigga you've only known for a couple of months. I love you, Keish, and ain't nobody gone take care of you like me. Have you even been taking your medicine? This nigga not gone give a damn about the shit that you got going on." I can't believe this dumb nigga was sitting here telling my business.

Dom was looking at me, trying to figure out what the fuck Mazzy was talking about.

"Shut the fuck up. I'm not going with you. Now leave me the fuck alone." I was sick of this nigga already. He grabbed my hand and tears fell from his eyes.

"Yo, is this nigga crying?" Dom questioned, and burst out laughing. This is what I'm talking about, this nigga is weak as fuck.

"Nigga, fuck you!" Mazzy gritted and held his gun on Dom. I jumped back, and Dom had this smirk on his face.

"Nigga, you done fucked up over a piece of pussy that don't even want your ass." Dom looked at Mazzy and pushed his way inside with his gun trained on us.

"Maz, you don't want to do this. Just leave and I swear nothing will happen to you," I said to him because I didn't want to see him get hurt. I just didn't want to be with him anymore, but I would tell him anything to get him out of here.

"Go get your shit and let's go." He didn't even look at me; his focus was on Dom.

"She ain't going no damn where with you." As soon as Dom said that shit, Mazzy hit him upside the head with the gun, and shit went left from there. Dom hit Maz, pulling his gun out and shooting his ass in the chest. I screamed out as I watched Maz bleed out.

"Go get your shit together, we're! We're leaving tonight. Fuckkkk!" Dom was pissed. I turned and walked down the hall to go do what he told me. I heard him on the phone, I guess he was calling somebody to come and get Mazzy's body out of his house. I can't believe Mazzy is dead. Why couldn't he just let shit be with his stupid ass? All he had to do was leave shit alone, and maybe one day, I would've come back to his ass.

The cleanup crew has been here for a couple of hours. I'm glad that Dom didn't have neighbors that were close by to hear the gunshots. He walked into the room and started throwing shit into his duffle bags.

"You got all your shit 'cause we gone be there for a minute? You said you got a crib for us to stay at, right?" Dom asked.

"Yeah, but they might be watching my house. I told you I did some shit that he would kill me over. I think we need to get a room and make our moves on the low." There was no way that we could stay at the place Maz and I was renting. Hell, the landlord probably changed the locks by now anyway, 'cause we damn sure haven't paid shit in months.

"Aight, my brother is coming with us. Let's get the fuck out of here, and when we get where we're going you gone tell me about this fuckin' medicine you're taking." He grabbed our bags and we walked out. It took us damn near seven hours to get to Philadelphia because we had to wait at the airport for the next flight to leave. We were tired as fuck and I knew we were going to sleep the day away. I have someone that is going to help us, and I'm happy as hell that I didn't burn all my bridges. Giving up a little pussy can take you a long way.

hings with me and Cas were back on track. I was still pissed about how this fuck boy thinks he gone just come to my shit and touch my girl. I was getting dressed to head over to my brother's househe. He just got back from New York not long ago. I haven't gotten around to telling him about the shit that went down at the club. Once I was dressed, I went downstairs in search of Cas. She was in her office, and I was so proud of my girl. She took this modeling shit with Zoe serious. These girls were making some bread off that shit. They were definitely making shit pop. I got a couple of surprises for Cas since her birthday is a week away, I was gonna give her a gift every day until her actual birthday.

"Yo, I'mma about to run over to Priest's crib for a lil'

minute." Cas was so busy on her computer; it took her ass a minute to respond to me.

"Ok, I'm surprised he came back so soon." Cas walked around the desk and stood in front of me, wrapping her arms around my waist.

"Yeah, I think he had some shit to handle. I think we should go to dinner tonight." I smiled at her.

"What Ms. Carol making for dinner?" She asked, just as I felt my phone vibrating in my hand. Looking at the text caused me to smile.

"Nahhh, this is not a Ms. Carol type a date. I want to take you out somewhere nice, just me and you. We been free-loading this whole damn relationship. I think I saved up enough money to take you somewhere nice." We both burst out laughing.

"Nigga, you right about that shit, but I loved every minute of that shit. I rather eat Ms. Carol cooking any damn day. I'm planning Zoey's baby shower in the backyard at Priest's house, and I'm thinking of having her make all of the food," she stated.

"That sounds like the move, babe come walk me out to my car." I had an early birthday gift for her, and I know her ass was gone be hype.

"Boyyyy, it's hot as hell out there, I will walk you to the door and shit. I don't feel like playing with the devil's ass today, so I plan on being inside for the rest of the day." I knew when she saw her gift, that shit was gone change her mind. We walked to the door, and I told her to go out first, I wanted her eyes to land on it first. When she saw that 2020 Mercedes Benz S Class black on black coupe, sitting there with the red bow on top, she looked at the car, and then back at me.

"Nas, whose car is that?" She asked with tears in her eyes.

"That's all you, lil mama, it's. It's for your birthday." She was stuck, so I grabbed her hand, and we walked to her car so she could take a look at it.

"You did this for me? I swear no one has ever done anything like this for me before. The only gifts I've ever received is from Zoey, and my mama," she cried, as she jumped into my arms.

"I love you, Bear, this is just the beginning, now. Now, get yoyo' ass down and enjoy your car. I will be back later." I kissed her lips and handed her the keys. Hopping in my car, I headed out to go check my brother out. Priest only lives about ten minutes from me, which was a good thing for my ass. Especially, when my ass was hungry and needed a damn meal. I used my key to get inside the house, Big mama was in the family room and Sasha was playing on the floor with her dolls.

"What's up, ole lady?" I asked her, kissing her on the cheek.

"Nothing much, just watching a little television. You talked to your daddy? I tried to call him last night and he didn't call me back," Big mama spoke.

"I talked to him yesterday, he over there trying to get to know the insides of stepmama. I told you they were doing the nasty the other day, and you're gonna have you a grandbaby soon." I burst out laughing because I know I need to cut that shit out. I loved telling them niggas' business to Big mama, that was my homegirl for real.

"Now you know they asses too old to be having a damn, baby. Speaking of that, Zoey 'bout to have your brother's, baby. I told her I'mma beat her ass after she haves that damn baby. All that talking we've been doing, and her ass didn't tell me she was pregnant," Big mama fussed.

"Yeah, but she had her reasons. I'm just glad they trying to work that shit out," I told her.

"I got something that's been bothering me, and I was gone talk to Priest about it. When that child got sick, you didn't find it strange that none of us was a match for her. Not even her mama and daddy was a match. I've been reading up on that shit. They say it's not uncommon for one of the parents not to match their child's blood type, but one of them would be a match. Some shit in the fuckin' water ain't clean. I'm sure that shit flew over our heads because we were concerned about saving her. I got my shit together now and had plenty of time to think about all the shit that's been going on with my family. I'm telling you now, all. All hell gone break loose if this baby is not his daughter."

"Who not whose daughter?" Priest questioned, walking into the room, and Big mama and I looked at each other.

"Grandson, sit down. I was talking to Nasir about when Sasha needed the transfusion. It was odd that none of us was a match for her, not even you and her mother. We may have missed it because we were concerned about her getting the blood she needed it. It's just been weighing heavy on me, and I think you need to look into it," Big mama told him. And for a long time, Priest just stared at her, not saying shit to us.

"Bruh, you good?" I asked him.

"You're saying you don't think Sasha is my daughter? That's my damn daughter, because if some shit comes out and says otherwise, I'm going back to jail. I will murder that bitch. I promise you I will rip her hoe ass heart out of her chest," he roared, and Sasha started crying. He picked her up and walked out of the room.

"Damn, this shit is crazy, but I feel you; something ain't right. I pray like hell that Big mama was wrong about this because this nigga was going to flip the fuck out, and so was I. That bitch was a fucked-up individual if she did some shit like that. I told Big mama I would check in on them later. I had to make a run to meet up with Cannon. I had him put it out that I was looking for this nigga Black. I should have been on my game when Cas said that was him at the club, I should have had my people put him on ice for me. I fucked that up, 'cause I was so focused on going off on my damn girl. I pulled up to the house out West and walked into the house.

"Where Cannon at?" I asked the workers that were bagging up the dope.

"He's in the back doing the count," Gerald spoke. I opened up the door to the office, and Cannon was on the phone.

"What up?" He stood to dap me up.

"You got a word on that nigga Black?" I asked him.

"Not yet, but we did get a location on both his sisters. I got somebody sitting on the spot, but nobody has been there in the last few days. They might be out of town, or he knows he fucked up and got them laying low. I should have something on his ass soon." I knew if I wanted a nigga found, Cannon was gone get the job done.

"That's good to know, did. Did you find out anything on that bitch Keisha?" I questioned.

"Yep, one of the guys said that Maz told him they were going to Atlanta. I put a bullet in his pussy ass for waiting so long to tell us that shit when we asked these niggas if they knew anything. I hate a bitch made nigga. I sent my cousin pictures of them and asked him to look into it for me. When they find them, we can jump on a plane and get at them niggas." I was with that shit. Priest wants their asses bad.

"Yo, what's up with you and Shericka, y'all? Y'all still getting married? I ain't heard you say shit about us getting fitted.."

"Nah, that's a wrap, the. The bitch cheating on me and as soon as she meets up with that nigga again, my ass gone be sitting in the midst waiting to put a bullet in both they asses." He shook his head.

"Damn, that's fucked up. I liked Shericka. She seemed so damn a wholesome, and shit." I looked at him with a smirk.

"Nigga, quit playing with me, we. We both know that bitch is a wholesome hoe. That goes to show you can't turn no hoe into a housewife. I knew better than to get that bitch out the strip club, but it was just something about the way she sucked my dick into that pussy of hers. That's what the fuck I get, my. My next bitch gone be green to this shit. I want me a bitch that's a nerd with big ass coke bottle glasses on her face," he laughed, this.

This nigga was as crazy as they came, but the bitches loved his ass. I dapped it up with him and called Cas to get ready for our date. By the time I pulled at home, Cas was walking out, and we got into her car. She wanted to drive me around tonight, and I damn sure let her. We decided to go to Ruth Chris Steakhouse out in King of Prussia.

"This is nice, babe. I already know what I want." She smiled, telling me what she wanted with her greedy ass. My girl and I were made for each other because we were both greedy as fuck, I loved that shit and her.

"Welcome to Ruth Chris what. What can I get you?" The waitress asked.

"We want two T-bone steaks and add some lobsters to that, and we will have the lobster mac & cheese, asparagus, and an order of crab cakes. We will also take a bottle of the house wine," I told them. Cas and I were enjoying our night out and after dinner, we decided to go have a few drinks at the club before we headed home.

Chapter Twenty-Six

KASH

 haven't been this happy in a long ass time, lately. Lately, my mind has been going back to my life with Bianca, and I feel this wave of guilt come over me. I think about Bianca and feel so fucked up that I've decided to move on, but what the fuck was I supposed to do. I have feelings for Eva, to the point that I want her ass with me every day. I damn near get an attitude when she has to leave and go home. To be honest, we gone have to do something about that shit asap.

"Kash, are you alright?" Eva asked, breaking me from my thoughts.

"I'm sorry, baby, did. Did you say something?" I questioned, smiling at her.

"I was saying that I have to go to the office, I should be back for dinner," she said.

"Ok, I will be down at the restaurant tonight. So, you can eat without me, or I can bring you some dinner home." Damn, this girl was fine. I was ready to put her ass back on her back. Ever since Eva and I got together, I have been inside of her ass every fuckin' day.

"I could just go back to my place tonight and stay the night with you tomorrow night." She smiled.

"Eva, don't fuckin' play with me, you. You know how I feel about you being here. We need to talk about that shit anyway. I want you here with me fulltime, I'm tired of you going back and forth." I needed her to really think about what I was saying to her.

"Kash, I think we should really think about that, it's. It's a big move for both of us. I would love to be here with you, but are you sure you're ready for that type of move? I know you're still healing from your wife, and I understand it. When I move in here, I want you to give me your heart fully."

"Eva, I will always love Bianca, that. That woman was apart of me for a long time we had a beautiful life together. She gave me my children, but me having love for her won't hinder what I feel in my heart for you. I never want you to feel like that when I'm with you. I'm not gonna lie to you; sometimes I feel guilty about starting over. I let that shit eat at me for over two years, and I can't do it anymore. I will block the woman that God has for me by doing that. I had to really do some soul searching about that shit. I made some bad moves with that chick Stormy. I know what I have with you is real, but I'm gone let you do you, baby. Whenever you ready, I will be right here waiting for you." I had to be honest with her, but I do understand her feelings and concerns.

"I hope you know you're stuck with me; it doesn't matter that we're in two different places. I belong to you, and I'm happy with what we have. No man has ever made me feel this way," she spoke, wrapping her arms around me. Kissing her on the lips, I grabbed her by the hands and walked her out to her car. The kiss we shared almost had me ready to slide in her ass right outside. Eva pulled away and turned to look around, with this funny look on her face.

"What's wrong?" I asked her.

"Nothing, I just had this feeling that someone was watching us," she laughed it off. I looked around to see if she was right, but there wasn't anybody that looked out of the ordinary.

"*N*ah, I don't think so, baby girl." I opened the car door for her.

"I think I just need to get some rest. I have had that feeling for a few days now," she stated.

"Pay attention to your surroundings, and if some shit starts to feel really off to you, call me." I don't want shit happening to her. Normally, when you get a feeling that some shit is off, nine times out of ten, that shit is fuckin off. I watched her drive off and went back into the house to relax for a while. I have been spending so much time with Eva that I haven't seen my family in a while. I sent a message to Nas, and Priest and told them to meet me at the restaurant for a couple of drinks. Tomorrow night is Cassie's birthday party at the club, and Eva and I plan on going. I haven't been out to party in a while, so I was looking forward to hanging out and having some fun. I'm hoping Zoey comes down for the party. I would love to see her. Cas is her cousin, so I'm sure she will be there. It was a little after eight when I made it down to my restaurant. Walking in, Lonnie was behind the bar making drinks.

"How is it going, boss?" He asked as I took a seat at the bar.

"Good, how is business tonight?" I looked around.

"Man, it's been busy all damn day." I laughed because Lonnie looked as if his ass was ready to tell everybody to get the fuck out. He placed a drink in front of me, just as Priest and Nas came walking in the door.

"Pop, I see you finally came up for some air. I know how it is when that pussy gets a hold of yo' ass. That shit will lock you down and put your ass in a chokehold," Nas laughed.

"Nigga, sit yo' ass down and get a drink," I laughed at his ass.

"What's up, Pop? It's good to see you, man." Priest dapped me up.

"Good to see you to, son. I heard you had to put a nigga on his ass in New York." I looked over at him.

"This nigga talk too much, but I got into a lil' something," Priest stated.

"Nigga, I didn't tell his ass shit! You need to ask him how

he knows so damn much; you will learn a lot. This the nigga that can probably get you and Zoe back together," Nas told him.

"What the hell is he talking about?" Priest questioned, looking over at his brother.

"Zoey told me what went down in New York. Zoey and I talk every night, we play online backgammon together," I said to him as I took a sip of my drink.

"You were the one she was on the phone arguing with about that game, every damn night that I was there? Her ass would keep me awake from all the loud talking and laughing she was doing," Priest said, shaking his head.

"Yep, give her some time, son, she. She loves you; she will come around soon enough," I told him. Zoey and I have had many talks about how she was feeling, and last night she told me that she still loved him. So, I knew eventually she will work her way back to him, it. It just takes time to heal from the hurt and pain.

"Yo, you Kash?" Some nigga questioned, walking up to us.

"What's up?" I asked him.

"Nigga, you took my fuckin' girl, and I'm here to let you know that I'm not going down like some sucka ass nigga!" This nigga yelled.

"Nigga, you need to calm yo lil' short syndrome looking ass down somewhere. Like where the fuck did you leave your height at the muthafuckin' crib, nigga? Coming up in here talking shit and yo' ass got the nerve to be the size of my muthafuckin' shoe," Nas said to him, as he and Priest both burst out laughing.

"Nigga, I can't take something you never had. You niggas kill me, you. You be too worried about getting the pussy when that's not all it is to a woman. You should be worried about learning her, learn what motivates her, know what her likes, and dislikes are. Getting pussy is a good thing, every man can appreciate some good pussy. Women like to be held, touched, cared for, loved on, not you sticking your no dick having ass in her acting like it's the best dick in the world.

Nigga, if you don't get the fuck out of my business with that shit! I assume you in my muthafuckin' face over Eva. I'm telling you now, don't fuck around and get yoyo' ass fucked up over a woman that doesn't belong to you. Be glad that I'm not tripping off this bullshit ass visit because I should beat your fuckin' ass right now. That's my muthafuckin' woman, and if I find out that you're fuckin' with her, I'm killing yoyo' ass."

"Ahhh, hell nawl! He up in here talking his shit over my stepmama? Nope, nigga, she taken," Nas dumb ass said to him, pulling his gun out and sitting it on the bar. I swear this boy was crazy and he loved himself some Eva. I guess that nigga didn't want no problems because he turned and walked out. This nigga lost his damn mind coming up in my shit, trying to fight for his girl like we a bunch of fuckin' teenagers in high school. If he fucks with Eva, he might as well go tell his mama to get her black dress picked out.

Chapter Twenty-Seven
CASSIE

*Y*esssss, today was my muthafuckin' birthday and I was in such a good mood. Shit was going good in my relationship with Nas. I'm so happy with this man. That shit with Black scared the shit out of me. I thought I was going to lose my man over that shit. I had to stand my ground with Nas because I didn't deserve that shit. He made me give up my place and move in with him. Throwing me out was not a fuckin' option, and I hated that I was even in a predicament like that. That's why it's always best that when you do some shit with a man, y'all do that shit together.

"Happy Birthday, Bear," Nas said, walking into the room with my breakfast and gifts. Every day up until my birthday, I got a gift from him, and I thought that shit was the sweetest thing ever. He really outdid himself, and I was to hype over this birthday. This is the first birthday in a long time that I felt completely happy and excited about the day.

"Awww thank you, babe." He bent down and kissed my lips. I opened the first gift and it was a Hermes bag. I opened the rest of my gifts, and I had purses, jewelry, clothes, and shoes. Everything he got me was either from Gucci, Louis Vuitton, and Fendi. Not to mention the hundred grand I pulled out of the purses my. My ass was up out of the bed ready to fuck all my thanks into his ass.

"Girl, get yoyo' nasty fine ass off me. I got another surprise for you. I need you to put some clothes on and come downstairs with me." I loved all of his gifts, so I was eager to get downstairs to see what else he had for me. I got up and took care of my hygiene real quick, putting on a pair of shorts and a tank top. Following him downstairs into the family room, I damn near lost my fuckin' mind. I was jumping and screaming like I was crazy. This was the first time my mom has ever come to visit me since I've been in Philadelphia.

"Oh my God, mom! I'm so happy to see you thank. Thank you for coming, mom," I excitedly spoke, hugging her, and kissing her cheek.

"Don't thank me; you need to thank my handsome son in law, right here. He called me up and paid for everything"." My mom smiled at Nas.

"Babe, this is the best birthday ever. You are really showing out today. I can't believe you did all of this for me, bringing my mom here just topped it all off for me." I smiled, this. This man was everything and I can't believe that he was doing all of this for me.

"Oh, I'm not finished yet. I need you two to go get freshened up; we got somewhere to go," he told us, with this goofy grin on his face. It took us about an hour to get dressed, and we were in the car and out the door. It seems that everywhere we go now, I always wanted to drive my car. I love this car, and my mom couldn't believe Nas got it for my birthday.

"After we go where we have to go, I'm going to take you ladies out for lunch." I looked at my man with the side-eye, knowing we were going to Priest's house for lunch.

"She's cooking something good for lunch?" I laughed.

"Girl, I'm not cheap all the time. We not going there. I think I'm gone take y'all to Bianca's; you know they food be slammin'." He knew damn well if we go to Bianca's we didn't have to pay for shit there. This man was a trip.

"You a fool, but I'm down for Bianca's," I told him, as we pulled up to this building.

"I know you been doing your thing, managing Zoe's career. I just thought I would help you along the way. Now you can start your own management company for models or whatever you want to do with it," he said, handing me the paperwork to the building, and the keys. I cried tears of happiness; I just couldn't believe what was going on right now.

"That's really nice, Nasir, thank. Thank you for taking care of my baby girl." My mom was just as surprised as I was.

"I will always take care of her; you will never have to worry about that. I have one more gift to give you right now, and the rest of your gifts I will give to you at your party. I know that shit that happened with Black, and our lil' spat made you feel some type of way. I don't ever want you to feel that the house we live in is just mine; that's our house. I was wrong as fuck for how I treated you so I made some changes to let you know that we're in this shit together, lil' mama." He handed me the document, and I wrapped my arms around him, crying my lil' ass off. Nas had my name placed on the deed of his house.

"Thank you, thank! Thank you so much. I love the hell out of you. If my mom wasn't here, I would fuck the shit out of you," I whispered in his ear.

"Ma, Cas over here trying to low key rape me," this nigga said to her laughing, and I popped his ass upside his damn head.

"Cas, leave my son alone," she laughed, patting Nas on the back.

"I love you too, babe, now. Now let's go grab some lunch." Nas, my mom, and I had the best time at Bianca's, and even Kash was there and he joined us for lunch. My mom was grinning in his damn face every two minutes. I had to let her know that he had a woman because homegirl was on it. Once we got back to the house, we relaxed, and I hopped on my man's dick to thank him for everything that he's done for me today. Hearing my phone ringing, I grabbed it off the nightstand.

"Hey, babe."

"Happy Birthday, bihhhhh!" Zoey sang into the phone.

"Thank you, babe. I saw that you called me, but my ass got sidetracked," I said to her.

"It's all good. I'm leaving in a couple of hours to come down. This will be my first time driving to the city, I've decided to stay at Priest's house while I'm there," she stated like he was gone let her stay anywhere else.

"Ummmm, that is to be expected. Guess what mom? Mom is here, and she's going to be here for a week. Nas surprised me and flew her up here." I knew Zoe was going to be hype.

"Really, oh? Oh my God, I can't wait to see her. Well, let me get myself together. I should be there by 8, and I will see you at the party. Love you, sis," she said and we ended the call.

———

*I*t was time for us to get dressed. Nas was in the shower because he was leaving to go to the club before us. He said he wanted to make sure everything was straight before everyone got there. I was so damn hype about my party tonight everyone. Everyone that was important to me would be there. Tiff and I talked, and she apologized for not hearing me out. I even told her my concerns about her lil' friend, and why I beat that bitch ass. She said she was gone look into that shit, and we would beat her ass together again. I laughed so damn hard at that silly ass girl, but she was dead ass serious. I have been feeling kind of bad for the last few days, and I was telling Zoey about it. Her ass immediately said that I was pregnant. I wasn't trying to hear that. It was the sickness that came over me this morning, that sent my ass to the store to get a test. I pulled it out of my purse and walked into the bathroom to take the test. Just as soon as I started pissing on the stick, Nas' ass was knocking on the door.

"Babe, I'm about to leave. Why the hell you got the door locked?" He questioned. I sat the test on the sink, washed my hands, and walked out of the bathroom.

"I didn't know it was locked. You're getting ready to head out?" I asked.

"Yeah, I wanted to tell you to pull your car in the back of the club. Call me when you get there, and someone will be out to get you and ma. Love you, I will see you later." He kissed my lips, and I followed him downstairs to go get me something to drink. Knowing that I had taken that test made my ass nervous.

"I will see you at the club in a lil' while, ma," Nas said to her.

"Alright, son." She hugged him, and Nas left out.

"Chile, you got yourself a good man. I'm so happy for you, baby." She smiled.

"Yeah, I love me some h...." I couldn't even finish my sentence because I thought I heard gunshots.

"Are those gunshots?" My mom asked, and my heart dropped. I ran to the window, and I could see Nas' car at the top of the driveway. I ran outside, running towards his car.

"Nas!" I screamed out in tears. Just as I made it to his car. I was being gripped up and thrown into a car. I was fighting, crying, and screaming because all I could think about is Nas' car being shot up. And me coming face to face with the devil himself.

Chapter Twenty-Eight

PRIEST

The shit that Big mama said to me a few days ago had me feeling fucked up, and my attitude has been crazy. I've been doing my best to keep my damn temper under control, but if this bitch done fucked around and did some shit like that to me and Sasha, I promise you her death is going to be a fuckin' massacre. I picked up my ringing phone and I saw that it was Zoe.

"Yeah," I spoke into the phone.

"Hey, I was just calling to let you know that I'm on my way." This would be the first time that she would be back in the house since all that bullshit with me went down. I'm glad she's coming because I wanted to talk to her.

"Ok, be careful, and I will see you when you get here. I will leave the gates opened, so you can just come on through."

I had my security systems changed out ever since I found that it was so damn easy to get into your shit with a keypad.

"Ok, I got about an hour to go. I will text you when I'm about twenty minutes out. See you soon," she stated, we. We talked for a little while longer and then ended the call. It was already after eight, so I know were going to get to the party late. Zoey still had to get dressed when she gets here. My phone was going off again, and I picked the call up.

"Hello," I spoke.

"Priest, it's Dr. Taylor. I just wanted to update you and let you know that my colleague is doing the DNA test for you right now. It's normally not how we do things, but I understand your concerns, and the payment you provided helped. We should have an answer for you within an hour," Dr. Taylor spoke.

"That's good to hear, I appreciate you doing this for me. As I told you before, I don't care what time it is just call me." That shit was weighing heavy on me, and I know that the hospital had my blood work, Keisha's, and Sasha's. So, I contacted Dr. Taylor in hopes that he would be able to give me some answers right away. I was disappointed to find out that he didn't have an answer for me. I told him that I would pay if he could get the test done for me quickly, and he worked it out for me. No matter what happens Sasha is my daughter, and that's the bottom line of that shit. I still want to know the truth. There was no way that I could go on with everyday life not knowing. I went down to the kitchen to grab a bite to eat before we started all of this partying and drink-ing. Big mama was in the kitchen, cutting her a slice a cake.

"Hey, grandson. What time you're heading out for the festivities?" She asked.

"I'm waiting on Zoey to get here and get dressed. She said she was about an hour away. How have you been feeling, you? You haven't been your feisty self these past couple of months?" I asked her. I wanted to make sure she was ok.

"It's just so much going on with my family; I've been praying for y'all nonstop. It's like the devil is working over-time on my babies, and it's weighing heavy on my heart. I just want y'all to be safe out there. It's so many evil ass people in this world. That ex-wife of yours is a piece of work. I just can't get over all the shit that her ass has put you through. Lawwwd, I know your mama is turning in her grave at all of this bullshit. Your damn daddy over there acting like he 18 and done forgot he got a damn mama. I guess it's a good thing that he's calling and checking on me again. That heifer sure must got some good snatch, 'cause she done snatched my damn son right on the hell up. That nigga is too far gone, me. Me and Nas going over there tomorrow to be noisy," she said, and I fell out laughing. Her and Nas' ass is always getting into some shit, and she's saying the shit like it's a good thing. I don't know if I should feel jealous of her, and Nas' relation-ship or be glad that it's not me that she likes to hang with.

"I thought you liked Eva?" I looked over at her.

"I do like her; I think she's a sweet girl. I just hope her ass ain't over there putting the roots on my damn son." Here she goes with that shit again.

"Big mama, don't start with the roots mess again." When I was married to Keisha, she swears she saw Keisha ass in the backyard burying something. She made me start flushing my hair out my brush and hide all of my pictures. I thought that was the craziest shit, but I did it for a couple of months just to please her.

"You keep thinking that shit a joke, but it's real, and that shit works. I just hope yo' daddy ain't a victim. Don't worry, your brother and I are gone get to the bottom of this shit, starting tomorrow." This lady was serious, and I'mma fuck Nas up for following her ass up. Big mama said she was going upstairs to watch television with Sasha. I decided to go ahead and get dressed for the party. It took me about an hour to get dressed, and Zoe ass still wasn't here. I called her phone, and she didn't answer, and just as I was about to call her again. She text me and said she had to stop and use the bathroom. She was about twenty minutes out. Walking downstairs to the family room, I decided to call Nas to let him know that I was waiting on Zoe, but he didn't answer his phone. Just as I hung up, Pop was calling me.

"What's up, Pop?"

"Son, Cassie's mom called down to the restaurant looking for me, she. She told Lonnie that something has happened to Nas and Cas. I'm on my way over there; I need you to get over there now!" My Pop yelled into the phone, just as I ended my call Dr. Taylor was calling me.

"Yeah," I spoke as I headed for the door.

"Priest, the DNA test showed that you're not Sasha's father," he said, and when I opened the door, I had two guns pointed in my face.

To Be Continued

UNTITLED

Get connected with Author K. Renee

To get VIP access of new releases, and sneak peeks please join my mailing list.

Text KRENEE to 22828

Website www.authorkrenee.com

Facebook: https://www.facebook.com/karen.renee.9421450

Instagram: http://www.instagram.com/Authorkrenee

Author K.Renee's Reading Group on FB: https://www.facebook.com/groups/1640789219356047/?ref=share

CPSIA information can be obtained
at www.ICGtesting.com
Printed in the USA
LVHW041736011020
667692LV00003B/448